Zombie King

Shifter Squad: Book 2

J.C. DIEM

Titles by J.C. Diem:

Mortis Series
Death Beckons
Death Embraces
Death Deceives
Death Devours
Death Betrays
Death Banishes
Death Returns
Death Conquers
Death Reigns

Shifter Squad Series
Seven Psychics
Zombie King
Dark Coven
Rogue Wolf
Corpse Thieves
Snake Charmer
Vampire Matriarch
Web Master
Hell Spawn

Hellscourge Series
Road To Hell
To Hell And Back
Hell Bound
Hell Bent
Hell To Pay
Hell Freezes Over
Hell Raider
Hell Hath No Fury
All Hell Breaks Loose

Fate's Warriors Trilogy
God Of Mischief
God Of Mayhem
God Of Malice

Loki's Exile Series
Exiled
Outcast
Forsaken
Destined

Hunter Elite Series
Hunting The Past
Hunting The Truth
Hunting A Master
Hunting For Death

Dedication:

To Paul and Shev – two of the most awesome people
I know.

Chapter One

Oppressive shadows crowded around the SUV as I waited for the gate to open. It began to close automatically once the vehicle was clear. The sky was overcast, which added to the general gloom, not to mention my sense of impending doom.

A series of twisting dirt roads eventually led me to the freeway. I didn't bother to use the navigation system as a guide. I'd made the trip many times during the past couple of months. The only difference this time was that I was behind the wheel.

The gloom remained with me until I left the base of the Rocky Mountains behind and hit the open road. Without the shadows of the range to act as a filter, the late afternoon sunlight was almost too bright.

Butterflies fluttered unpleasantly in my stomach. I'd been feeling decidedly queasy ever since I'd called my father a couple of nights ago. My dad was a highly trained army sniper and he was frequently deployed on overseas missions. Three long months had passed since I'd last seen him. That might be unusual for most families, but it was normal for us. The only reason he was even returning to the US right now was to check up on me, and possibly to murder my boss.

It felt strange to be making the long journey to the Denver International Airport on my own. I'd rarely had a chance to be alone since leaving Texas. Mark had agreed that it was probably a good idea for me to pick up my dad solo rather than to take the entire squad with me. Even I didn't know how my father was going to react when he met the team for the first time.

A lot had changed since he had last seen me. Agent Mark Steel had temporarily needed a sharpshooter on his team to help combat some very dangerous people. My dad, Major Philip Levine, was the best. Unfortunately, he'd been unavailable and my assistance had been requested in his absence. I'd only been allowed to tag along on the mission because Mark had promised to keep me safe.

A federal agent for the highly secretive Paranormal Investigation Agency, Mark headed a small team known as the TAK Squad. They'd been hunting seven psychopathic psychics and I was to be their backup if anything went wrong. Something had indeed gone wrong and I'd learned the hard way that the Track and Kill Squad were far more than they'd seemed.

Agent Reece Garrett, second in charge of the team, had fallen beneath the spell of one of the psychics. Her nickname was Lust and she'd been named that with good reason. Deeply perverted, she had two favorite tricks. One was to compel people to have sex with whomever they desired the least. Her other trick was to force her victims into sleeping with the person who desired *them* the least. I couldn't decide which compulsion was worse.

It was no secret that Reece found me to be an annoyance. Well aware that I had a crush on him, he'd flat out told me that he wasn't interested in me. His rejection had hurt, but it hadn't come as a surprise. Based on how little attraction he felt towards me, it had been a shock when he'd burst into the compound one night with the intention of getting naked with me.

I'd come to the conclusion that Lust had ordered him to sleep with the person he least wanted to become intimate with; me. That realization hadn't done much to bolster my already fragile self-esteem.

Being forced to endure Lust's compulsion had only been the start of a problem that we now both shared. It had been the worst possible time for him to succumb to the telepath's order. It had been the first night of a full moon and he'd bitten me during the process of taking my virginity.

I hadn't told anyone that we'd briefly been lovers. I'd planned on taking that information with me to the grave. That decision had been taken out of my hands four weeks later when the full moon had risen again and I'd turned into a creature of myth.

Mark knew that something had gone awry when I'd disappeared for three nights in a row. When I'd returned to the compound, he'd called Reece and me together and asked me what had happened between us on the night of my eighteenth birthday. My mortified expression had been answer enough. He'd then asked me if I'd been bitten. The horror that Reece had felt when he'd realized what he'd done to me was burned into my memory. It wasn't going to fade anytime soon.

I'd had the greatest shock of my young life when Mark explained to me that the bite hadn't just scarred my shoulder. I'd contracted a virus that turned me into a werewolf with every full moon. The scar was undeniable proof that I'd been marked. It was a permanent reminder of the events that only I could recall.

That kind of secret couldn't be kept from my dad and I'd broken the news to him over the phone two nights ago. He'd immediately left whatever assignment he'd been on and had headed home. He'd called late last night to advise me that he'd be landing in Denver this afternoon. Now here I was, on my way to pick him up. I hoped I'd be able to calm him down during the drive back to the compound. He was slow to anger, but once his ire was roused, whoever had incensed him would be best advised to duck and run.

I paid only cursory attention to the scenery during the long drive. The pine and birch trees became fewer and fewer until they eventually petered out altogether. When they did, open fields took over. Traffic became much denser when I passed through Denver. It took almost two and a half hours before I finally reached the airport.

Parking as close as I could get to the terminal, I went the rest of the way on foot. I'd dressed inconspicuously in jeans and a white t-shirt. My blue leather jacket hid the gun holster that I wore on my left side. It seemed like a good idea to leave the Beretta in the car. It would be safe enough hidden beneath the seat until I returned. The SUV was all but impenetrable. No ordinary car thief would be able to break into it.

I was aware of men staring at me when I entered the building and hurried towards the gate where my dad would be arriving at any minute. At five foot seven, I was slender and had long black hair and dark brown eyes. I looked a lot like my mother, not that I actually remembered her. She'd died when I was only a few months old.

My father had given me a silver locket on my fifth birthday. A photo of my mother was on the left side and a picture of me was on the right. She'd been in her early twenties when the photo had been taken and I'd been just an infant. Afraid of losing or damaging the locket, I usually kept it in a small pewter jewelry box. It held the few items of jewelry that I'd collected over the years. I'd rarely worn the locket simply because it was so precious to me.

A few months had passed since I'd looked at my mother's photo, but I remembered it well enough. We both had oval faces and the same nose, eyes and mouths. We even shared the same shallow cleft in our chins. She'd been born somewhere in Europe, which explained her exotic looks. Her features were finer than mine and I'd never be as beautiful as she'd been.

Forgetting that shifters were allergic to silver, I'd made the mistake of picking up the locket before leaving the compound this morning. My fingers still stung from touching the chain. The burns on my skin would take several hours to heal. I'd have to put gloves on if I wanted to open the locket again. I'd never be able to wear it now. The only memento that I had of my mother was almost inaccessible to me.

My dad didn't like to talk about his late wife. Bringing up her memory was always painful for both of us, so we rarely discussed her. I knew she'd been murdered, but not who had been responsible or if they'd ever been caught. I couldn't imagine my father allowing the killer to escape. I could easily imagine him hunting the guy down, putting a bullet in the back of his head and burying his body where it would never be found.

A couple of guys not much older than me turned to stare and one of them whistled beneath his breath. It should have been too quiet for me to detect, but my hearing was far more acute now. The pair was staring not just because they thought I was pretty, but because of my new and unusual grace. Before I'd become a shape shifter, I'd been just as clumsy as any other teen. I was now stronger, faster and I could tear people's limbs off with my bare hands if they made the mistake of threatening me.

Reaching the correct gate, I jostled for position among the crowd as we waited for our friends and family members to arrive. I spied my dad straight away as the passengers began to straggle out through the gate. Dressed in tan cargo pants and a white t-shirt, he was six foot four and towered over most people. His dark blond hair was beginning to turn gray at the temples. He was only forty-five, but his face was weathered from spending so much time outdoors. His eyes were light blue and they were weary from nearly two solid days of travelling. We didn't look anything alike and it was sometimes hard to believe that we were even related.

My dad picked me out of the crowd and a stab of pain lanced through my chest at his wary expression. Then he smiled and opened his arms and my anguish disappeared. I might turn into a monster for three nights out of every month, but I was still his little girl.

I was careful not to move too quickly as I ran towards my father and threw myself into his arms. He caught me as if I was five years old rather than a fully grown adult. Lifting me off the ground, he hugged me tightly, then planted a kiss on my brow. "I've missed you, kiddo," he said as he put me down.

I hadn't changed much on the surface. The most dramatic changes had occurred on the inside. "I've missed you, too," I said and slipped my arm through his. There were too many people standing around for us to discuss my problem openly. We headed for baggage claim in a companionable silence. He'd already gone through customs when he'd first landed in L.A. so he didn't have to endure that long and boring process again.

His suitcase was easy to identify. It was the only one that looked like it had been through a war zone. Small, brown and scuffed, it could hold enough clothing for a week. While I was glad to see my dad again, I wasn't sure it would be a good idea for him to stay for that long. The more time he spent with the team, the greater his urge to murder them might become. Especially once I told him the details of how I'd become a shape shifter. We'd skipped the talk about the birds and the bees, to our mutual relief and we'd never discussed sex before. I'd learned everything I needed to know at school and in books. I wasn't looking forward to talking about this particular topic with my only remaining parent.

He waited until we were in the sleek black SUV before turning to me. "Tell me everything that happened to you after Agent Steel took custody of you."

Wrinkling my nose at his choice of words, I didn't argue that Mark had been in charge of my welfare. Technically, he'd been my guardian until I'd turned eighteen. I'd passed that milestone on the same night that I'd been bitten by Reece. Now Mark was my boss, which was still a bit of a shock. I'd gone from being an ordinary teenager to a supernatural secret agent in the space of two months.

As quickly and concisely as I could, I told my father about our hunt for the Seven Deadly Sinners. That was the nickname that the team had given to the telepaths. I reached the part where Reece had burst into the base and had looked up at me with feral golden eyes and I ran out of words. The events that had happened after that had been both frightening and exciting. While my physical pleasure had been memorable, it had ultimately resulted in me being turned into a monster.

I'd described the effect that Lust had on her victims so I wouldn't have to tell him in detail what had transpired that night. Reading between the lines, my dad crossed his arms when I fell silent. I was glad I was driving for a change. He was both weary and furious, which wasn't a good combination when you were behind the wheel. "Did he hurt you?" he asked tightly.

As far as he knew, I'd been an innocent before I'd become a member of the TAK Squad. "No," I said. "I was frightened, but he didn't hurt me." He winced and I offered him a sympathetic look. It couldn't be easy listening to my story as my father. "It wasn't Agent Garrett's fault," I said. "Shifters apparently have a natural resistance to mind control, but the telepath was too strong for even him to resist. He'd have died if he hadn't obeyed her order."

Turning to study me, what he said next didn't particularly surprise me. "You know which outcome I'd have preferred," he said and it was my turn to flinch. He knew me well and he figured there was something that I wasn't telling him. "You have feelings for him," he said with heavy certainty.

Sighing at his perceptiveness, I nodded. "Yeah, I do." I laughed and it sounded far too mature and cynical for someone of my age. "He doesn't even remember what happened between us. Just like I don't remember the second time I…" I trailed off, realizing what I'd been about to divulge.

"This happened to you more than once?" he asked, outraged on my behalf. "Was it the same guy?"

Misery that I'd tried hard to suppress came back and I shrugged. "I don't know who it was. I made the mistake of trying to hunt Lust down on my own and I got too close to her. She must have given me an order to sleep with someone just before Garrett arrived and scared her off." Being around my dad brought back my habit of referring to people by their rank or surname. I'd mostly broken myself of that habit lately.

"I apparently managed to get away from him during the drive back to our base," I continued. "It was the first night of the full moon and it was also the first time that I changed into a werewolf. I don't remember anything for three nights. I woke up in the forest near the base and found my way back to the compound." I didn't think it would be a good idea to tell him that I'd woken up naked and covered in blood. I definitely wasn't going to mention my shredded underwear.

"Are you sure you had intercourse with a second man?" he asked and looked pained at what I'd presumably gone through.

"I must have," I replied bleakly. "Otherwise, I'd be dead." Catastrophic brain failure was the result if a victim of the telepaths failed to follow through on the orders that they were given. The fact that I was still alive was proof enough that I'd been intimate with someone.

I'd been trying hard not to think about who I'd given my body to just five nights ago. There was only so much I could take before I'd break and I felt like I was already teetering on the edge. It wouldn't take much more to push me over.

Chapter Two

My father went silent when I finished telling him everything that had happened to me while he'd been overseas. Taking quick sidelong looks at him, I could tell that he was blaming himself. As far as I knew, he'd never regretted his job before, but he might very well be regretting it now. If he'd been home, none of this would have happened. Not that I held him accountable for any of it.

I'd been only seventeen and had still been a minor when I'd agreed to assist Mark and his team. I was now an adult but I almost felt as if my childhood had been stolen away from me. I'd never be the same innocent young teen again.

We passed the final hour of our journey mostly in silence. I didn't know what was going to happen once we reached the compound. I suspected that my dad wasn't going to be able to control his temper. He was almost vibrating with anger and he was breathing faster than normal. I was astounded to realize that I could hear his rapid heartbeat.

All of my senses had become enhanced after I'd been bitten. Now that I'd become something other than human, my sense of hearing, smell, sight and taste were much stronger than usual. Just like my fellow squad members, I'd be able to track my quarry from their scent alone. My enhanced senses were useful tools, but I wasn't sure that they outweighed the downside that I was now essentially a monster.

The sun had set sometime during our journey and it was fully dark by the time we reached the base of the mountains. I turned off onto the lesser used road and eventually took the dirt track that led to the compound. When I stopped at the gate, my father peered upwards through the windscreen at the thirty foot high steel fence that was tipped with razor wire. The electrified barrier looked almost strong enough to imprison an elephant. I took a small remote control device out of my pocket, pressed a button and the gate swung open. The SUV became enclosed by trees as we wended our way along a narrow track.

A wide, two story concrete building appeared through a break in the trees. While I could see it quite clearly, only the single light shining near the garage enabled my dad to view it. Plain and austere, at first glance it looked like the lair of an evil genius. Even at a second glance, it was still imposing.

The same device opened the garage door and I turned the SUV around so I could reverse it inside. Apart from a black van to our left, the spacious garage was empty. There was enough room for ten cars and our two vehicles looked almost lonely sitting side by side.

Before I climbed out, I snagged my gun from beneath the seat and slid it back into its holster. My dad followed me to the reinforced metal door that required a palm scan to open it. Mounted on the wall next to the door, the device came to life when my hand touched it. Green light shone brightly as my prints were examined and accepted.

We stepped into a hallway that stretched out to the right with intermittent doorways on each side. There was only one door to the left and another scanner waited. The compound had scanners on all but the bedroom doors.

Before opening the door, I assessed my father's mood. His lips were pinched into a thin line, but he seemed stable enough. "Promise me you won't kill anyone," I said with my hand hovering over the scanner.

He looked down at me without saying anything. I could be just as stubborn as him and I cocked my eyebrow to indicate that I could stand there all night if I had to.

Scowling slightly, he finally gave in and nodded. "You have my word that I won't kill anyone." I heard the unspoken 'yet' behind his pledge and knew it was as good as I was going to get. If he'd been armed, I wouldn't have opened the door at all. Since his weapons were presumably back in whatever country he'd just left, I figured the team would have a small chance of fleeing before he could take my gun away from me and use it on them.

The door unlocked when my prints were accepted again and I pushed it open. My dad flicked a quick look around, cataloging everything in sight. To the right was a boxing ring and gym. A spiral staircase sat in the middle of the room and led to the coms area and bedrooms upstairs. To the left were the living area, dining room and kitchen at the back.

The rest of the team was seated on the three U-shaped black leather couches in the living room. Trepidation was apparent in their posture. All four agents stood when we stepped inside.

"Dad, this is Agent Kala Walker," I pointed at the pretty and vivacious blond with short, spiky tawny golden hair. Kala was of medium height and build and had a solid frame rather than a waifish one like mine. She gave my father a quick nod and the once over. He cut an impressive figure and her interest reminded me that women found him to be attractive. After losing my mother, he'd dedicated his life to his job and to raising me. He hadn't had the time or inclination to date anyone else. If he'd had any encounters of the carnal nature, he'd kept them well hidden from me.

"Next to her is Agent Flynn Bailey." Flynn was only a couple of inches shorter than my dad, but more slender. He was from a mixed heritage with mocha colored skin and green eyes. He kept his black hair cut very short. He also offered my father a nod of greeting and respect.

"This is Agent Reece Garrett," I said and nodded to the third young agent. He was just under six feet tall, had wide shoulders, a ripped body, a gorgeous face, dark brown hair and brown eyes that were a few shades lighter than my own. Not that I'd spent much time drooling over him.

Keeping his expression blank, my father turned his attention to the man who had changed my life so drastically. Reece wasn't as practiced at hiding his emotions and he swallowed nervously. It couldn't have been easy facing the father of the girl you'd turned into a monster.

Before the silence could become even more uncomfortable, I finished the introductions. "You already know Agent Steel, of course," I finished up. Mark was in his mid-forties and had receding brown hair and gray eyes. Exactly how they knew each other was still a mystery to me. I hoped I'd learn the answer to that question eventually. It would probably be a very interesting story.

Mark quailed when he saw murder in my father's now chilly eyes. Reece, Kala and Flynn instinctively moved to shield our boss from the approaching soldier. "It's okay," he said and stepped out from concealment. "I'll take whatever punishment the Major deems fit." He rounded the couches and came to a stop in front of us.

My dad didn't hesitate to deal out said punishment. His fist rammed into Agent Steel's face and sent him crashing to the floor.

Reece was the first to react. With a snarl of rage, he leaped over the couch and landed lightly in front of us. I moved even faster and pushed my father out of the way. With blinding speed, my hand dipped beneath my jacket and I drew my gun.

Staring down the barrel of my Beretta, he showed grudging admiration. I'd been fast before my change, but now I was lightning. "You have a bad habit of pointing your gun at my face," he said evenly.

"You have a bad habit of making me want to shoot you," I countered. I sensed no fright from him at all. He knew that I wasn't going to shoot him. I might have killed two of the psychics during the course of our mission, but I hadn't become a trigger happy psychopath. I'd only shoot if my father's life was in danger.

Climbing to his feet, my dad rubbed his arm where I'd shoved him. My strength was a little frightening now and he was trying hard not to back away from me. I'd never seen him so spooked before and it saddened me that I was the cause of his fear.

Kala and Flynn helped Mark to his feet and he held a handkerchief to his bleeding nose. "Reece, Alexis," he warned us in a low, calm voice. "Stand down."

I waited for the tension to seep out of Reece's shoulders before I even contemplated putting my gun away. As always, Mark wore a dark suit that identified him as being a federal agent. All three of his agents wore a white t-shirt and camouflage cargo pants. When I'd first arrived at the compound, Reece had usually been shirtless. Since two nights ago, he'd begun wearing a t-shirt. I didn't know why, but I suspected it had something to do with me. Maybe he'd grown tired of me ogling his half naked body. I was working on toning down my need to stare at him, but he was handsome enough to turn most female's heads.

My dad's hand came to rest on my shoulder. "Put the gun away, Lexi. If anyone is going to do the shooting around here, it'll be me."

I slipped my weapon back into its holster, but I kept a wary eye on the other three shape shifters. They didn't like their guardian being attacked and all were now hostile towards my dad.

"Now that you've gotten that out of your system," Mark said wryly, "do you think we can talk without causing each other any further physical damage?" He checked the handkerchief to see if the bleeding had stopped. It had, so he tucked the stained fabric into his pocket.

My father gave a single, short nod and pointed at Kala and Flynn. "You two can leave." Reece shifted his weight and drew my father's attention to him. "*You* stay put," he said in a tone that brooked no argument.

Looking to our boss for guidance, Kala and Flynn waited for his nod before they headed for the kitchen door that led to the front of the compound. Neither were happy about leaving, but little would be resolved if they stayed.

"I trusted you with my daughter's welfare," my father said tightly to Mark once the two shifters were gone. "You gave me your word that Alexis would be safe."

His tone was one step short of being vicious and Mark put a calming hand on Reece's shoulder to stop him from reacting to the perceived threat. My father was coiled violence waiting to happen and he was even more deadly than us non-humans. "I know," Mark said softly. "I'm deeply sorry for what happened to Lexi." His apology was sincere, but my dad would see it as being too little, too late.

"Lexi's condition is my fault, Major Levine," Reece confessed. He unconsciously straightened his spine when my father turned his attention to him again. "I got too close to the target and fell under her compulsion. This would never have happened to your daughter if I'd been more careful."

Beneath my own pain and embarrassment, I could see his misery. He cast an anguished look at me and I had to look away before my eyes filled with tears. His unhappiness and self-loathing were palpable. "I take full responsibility and I'm willing to step up and do the right thing," he said. A surge of astonishment and alarm in the back of my head told me he hadn't planned on saying this. He was almost as astounded as the rest of us by his pronouncement.

"What do you think would be the right thing to do in this situation?" my father asked. His tone was difficult to interpret. If I had to guess, I'd say he was torn between fury and exasperation.

"Marriage," Reece forced out and his normally tanned face went white. He ran a hand through his short Mohawk, giving away his nervousness.

Outraged by his stupidity, I was about to deliver a furious tirade, but my father held up his hand to stop me. "Exactly, which century do you think we're living in, son?" he asked with a hint of incredulity. "Just because you had intercourse with my daughter does not mean that she should be forced to tie herself to you for the rest of her life." He had strong views about marriage and believed it should only be undertaken if the couple were sure that they were compatible.

He glanced at me to judge my reaction and I gave him a nod of approval. I was more than capable of standing up for myself, but he wasn't going to let this kind of idiocy slide. "What about the second man she had relations with?" he asked and I suddenly wished I hadn't given him my consent to continue. "Should she marry him, too? Maybe you two can fight it out and Lexi can marry the victor." His sarcasm was cutting enough for both agents to wince. While amused that my dad couldn't bring himself to use the word 'sex' in relation to me, I cringed at him bringing up the second, unknown man that I'd been forced to satisfy sexually.

"What second man?" Mark asked, thoroughly confused by the turn of conversation.

"Lexi has reason to believe that the psychic ordered her to be intimate with someone when she went after her on her own," my father ground out. He sent a stern glance at me for putting myself in unnecessary danger. "She advised me that she'd have died if she didn't obey the command. Since she's still alive, we can only assume that she had intercourse with someone."

"There was no second man," Reece said into the awkward silence that followed that revelation.

He stared down at his feet rather than meeting my eyes and I knew he felt my shock. My mind went blank in surprise for a moment. "There had to have been. My brain would have melted otherwise." It wouldn't have literally melted, but it would have felt like it. A complete neural collapse wasn't pleasant. I'd seen the brain scans and video footage of several victims to prove it.

"I thought you said you found Lexi before the psychic could give her any commands," Mark accused his agent. He didn't like being lied to and expected better from his team.

"I lied to protect her," Reece confessed and withered a little at the betrayal on my face and in my heart. "I didn't want anyone to know what she'd been forced to do. Again," he added unhappily.

"How do we know you're telling us the truth now?" my dad asked. "How do we know she didn't find someone else to fulfill the compulsion with?"

Reece pulled his shirt away from his neck to reveal a still healing bite mark on his left shoulder. "If a human had bitten me, this would have healed straight away," he said. "This scar is going to be permanent and it could only have been made by another shifter."

I touched the bite mark on my left shoulder and I couldn't stop my eyes from filling with tears this time. We'd both always carry the marks as a reminder that we'd been forced to sleep together. Now I knew why he'd taken to wearing a shirt again. He'd been too ashamed to let anyone see it and discover what I'd done to him.

"You said that Lust commanded you to have sex with me," he said. "I couldn't let you die." He reached out a hand towards me, but I shook my head then turned and fled. I'd reached my breaking point and nothing was going to stop me from falling into an emotional abyss.

Chapter Three

Mortification flooded through me as I slapped my hand on the scanner. The door unlocked and I sprinted down the hall to the exit at the far end. Kala and Flynn were somewhere out the front of the compound and I needed to be alone.

The outdoor gun range beckoned and I didn't stop running until I'd reached the field. Dropping to my knees, I sobbed out my heartache. It had been bad enough when I thought I'd had intercourse with a total stranger, but this was somehow worse. Even if Reece didn't remember our first time, it was forever burned into my memory. The revelation that we'd had sex twice now was humiliating and my self-esteem plummeted even further. I'd never even know what our second time had been like.

When I'd finally sobbed myself out, footsteps alerted me that someone was approaching. I didn't need to turn around to know it was my father. I could smell his cologne from three hundred yards away.

There was enough moonlight shining on the path to guide him to me safely. He hunkered down and put a hand on my back. "Are you okay?" he asked.

"No," I replied. My voice was thick with tears. "I don't think I'll ever be okay again." It came out sounding more melodramatic than I'd intended, but it was too late to take the words back now. I was supposed to be an adult, but I sounded like a wounded little girl.

My misery was no doubt hurting my dad as well, but he couldn't fix this for me. As far as I knew, there was no cure for lycanthropy. "Do you want me to shoot him?" he offered hopefully.

I was pretty sure he was kidding and uttered a pained laugh. "If I wanted him dead, I'd kill him myself."

"That's my girl." He patted me on the back then helped me to stand. "What did you think of Agent Garrett's proposal?"

My laugh was more genuine this time, and a trifle horrified as well. "Where did that even come from? No one gets married just because they've had sex anymore."

"Mark has a theory about why the kid made the offer," my father said.

Something told me this could only be more bad news. "I can't wait to hear this," I muttered wearily.

"He thinks the two of you have bonded." My expression reflected my puzzlement, so he explained further. "Apparently, biting during intercourse between werewolves can sometimes lead to them becoming mated."

I didn't like the sound of that at all. It seemed far too permanent. Mark had better have a good explanation for this or someone really was going to end up full of bullets.

Kala and Flynn had returned to the building by the time we entered the living room again. Mark had filled them in on everything that they'd missed while I'd been falling apart at the gun range.

Kala gave me an assessing glance, then stepped over and put her arm around my shoulder. "Being mated to Garrett won't be so bad," she whispered. "You'll get to have sex with the eye candy as often as you like." Flynn doubled over with laughter and Reece went bright red. Mark and my father hadn't heard the exchange and they stared at us strangely, unaware of the joke.

"There will be no bonding and no more sex," I said loudly enough for everyone to be able to hear me, including the humans.

"I'm afraid the bond has already happened and it can't be reversed," Mark said apologetically. "Reece can already sense you." He watched my pale face become whiter as all of the color drained away. "Have you felt him in your head yet?"

"No!" I said more forcefully than I'd meant to. "I haven't felt anything at all," I lied. I was so embarrassed by this whole thing that I couldn't even bring myself to look at Reece.

"How much do you know about bonding?" my dad asked Mark.

He shook his head. "Not much, I'm afraid. There is very little information about shape shifters in the PIA records. I've heard rumors, but I can't substantiate them. I've read that this kind of bonding is rare and usually only happens between alpha couples."

All eyes swung from Reece, to me and back to Mark again. "You think Lexi is an alpha?" Kala said incredulously. I couldn't help but share her doubt. While I was far from meek, I'd never shown leadership tendencies before.

"She's young," Mark replied with a shrug. "Lexi only turned eighteen a little over a month ago and she's very new to being a shifter. Time will tell whether she turns out to be an alpha or not."

"What happens if I do turn into an alpha?" I asked.

Kala was the one to answer me. "Then we'd better go shopping for a wedding dress." Her grin was playful, yet I didn't find anything funny about this situation. I went lightheaded at the mental picture of walking down the aisle in a frilly white dress.

My father steadied me with a hand on my elbow. I was immensely grateful for his presence and I wasn't sure that I could have gotten through this without him. "My offer still stands," he leaned down to whisper to me.

He'd probably feel no guilt at all at shooting the man who had deflowered me and had turned me into a werewolf. "I'll keep it in mind," I muttered. Reece had changed my life forever, but I didn't want to see him hurt. It hadn't been his choice to bond with me, it had just been an accident and he clearly regretted it. I wasn't the only one who was going to suffer. He shared my misery.

"I'm beat," my father said. "I haven't had much sleep for the past couple of nights and I could use a few hours of rest."

"You can take the first bedroom on the left upstairs," Mark said. It was a spare room and wasn't currently in use.

I escorted my dad up to the second floor and he gave me a hard hug that made my ribs creak in protest. "I love you, honey," he said before stepping inside.

"I love you, too, Dad," I whispered to the closed door and trudged back downstairs, passing Mark in the coms room on the way.

Kala was making coffee in the kitchen as I took a seat on the couch. She carried two mugs into the living room, put them on the coffee table then sat beside me close enough for our shoulders to rub together. Reece and Flynn were sparring in the boxing ring, working off their excess energy caused by tension. All in all, the meeting had gone well. Everyone was still alive and they were still in possession of all of their limbs. I'd expected more bloodshed than just one small nosebleed.

Flicking a glance over her shoulder, the vivacious blond leaned in to speak to me. "Now I get why you were asking me about what sex feels like," she whispered just loudly enough for me to hear her.

"This is all so embarrassing," I whispered back. I put my hands over my face in despair.

"There are no secrets in the Shifter Squad," she replied. I could feel her studying me. Shifter Squad was our private name for the team and it was extremely apt. "Remember when you were asking about feeling heat during orgasm?"

My face glowed red and I dropped my hands and nodded. "As if I could forget."

"I'm pretty sure that only happened because Garrett marked you."

"The heat had already started before he bit me," I argued.

"Oh." Kala's defeat only lasted for a second. "Then there can only be one explanation."

Already wary about her theory, I lifted my eyebrow. "Do tell."

"You two were meant for each other."

Her tawny eyes all but sparkled with amusement and I groaned loudly enough for the guys to glance over at us. "That is so corny!" I complained. "You sound like something out of a paranormal romance book."

"Do you read many of those?" she asked curiously.

"Sometimes," I confessed and we shared a giggle.

Lost in thought, I stared at the TV without seeing it as Kala switched on a movie. I'd lied when I'd said that I didn't sense Reece. I'd thought it was all in my mind when I'd first noticed a different set of emotions in the back of my head. It had started right after I'd woken up naked in the woods and now it was impossible to deny. Even without looking at him, I could point to wherever he was. Right now, I sensed that he was fluctuating between feeling self-loathing and the urge to run away. He thought it would help if we didn't have to see each other every day, but he was wrong. We'd still be tied together, even if we moved far enough away that we couldn't sense each other at all.

At least I'd regained my taste for coffee. Apparently, our sense of taste went wonky right before and after we changed. Most of the time, we could pass for normal. It was only when we moved too fast or revealed just how good our senses were that we were in danger of being noticed. I'd have to practice something I'd never had to think about before; being human.

Chapter Four

My father's impromptu vacation only lasted for three days before he was called back to work. Tensions had been running high in the compound. We were all relieved when his commanding officer had ordered him to return to his mission. I had no idea who he was hunting and knew better than to ask. My dad had seen that I was alive and physically well for himself and he'd come to the conclusion that there was nothing he could do to help me. His emotional support had been welcome and I was glad he'd managed to take the time off to see me.

We'd had several long talks and he felt slightly better about my situation now. My transformation into a monster wasn't all bad. According to my new boss, I was now impervious to disease and illness.

The obvious downside was that I turned into a ravenous beast for three nights out of a twenty-eight day cycle.

Mark had checked that no one had gone missing while I'd been in my beast form. If I'd eaten a human, he'd have had no choice but to execute me. Shape shifters were tolerated as long as they hadn't taken a human life. Once they had, they developed a taste for killing humans and had to be destroyed. An extra enclosure was already being erected to contain me. It would be completed in time for me to be locked up when the moon became full again less than three weeks from now. I wasn't happy about being held prisoner, but the enclosure was my best chance of remaining alive. Besides, I wouldn't even remember being held captive.

"You'll call me if you need me?" my dad asked for the fifth time as I pulled up out front of the airport. Once again, I'd made the trip without my team mates. They could be overprotective at times, but none had complained about my decision to go alone. They knew I needed time to acclimatize to my new status as a shifter. It would be nice to have a couple of hours to myself during the journey back to our base.

"You'll be the first one I call if I need help," I replied. Not that he could possibly reach me in time if I really did need him. He was going back to wherever he'd been deployed, and I wouldn't see him for weeks or possibly even months. "I'll be fine. You should go or you'll miss your flight."

He studied my face and I strove to appear calm and relaxed. He'd given me as much moral support as he could considering we were both still in shock at the changes that I'd undergone. We were both still coming to terms with me being a werewolf and also with me being bonded to the man who had turned me. "Take care of yourself, kiddo," he said and leaned over to hug me.

"I promise I'll try not to eat anyone," I said mockingly and received a narrow-eyed stare in return. He climbed out, retrieved his suitcase from the backseat then saluted me and disappeared into the terminal.

Now that I was alone again, I waited for the tears to flow. Nothing happened and I started when a horn beeped as a car pulled up behind me, urging me to move. Putting the SUV into gear, I drove away from the airport.

Music played softly in the background and I contemplated my future as I drove back to the base. Now that I was a permanent member of the TAK Squad, Mark would probably want me to refine my skills. That meant I'd have to spend time with the entire team, which didn't fill me with joy. Reece had barely spoken to me during the past few days and he couldn't even look me in the eye most of the time.

Fresh shame and embarrassment swept through me. It was torture to be so close to him, knowing that he'd had to force himself to sleep with me twice. Okay, the first time it had happened he'd definitely enjoyed himself. But he'd only touched me in the first place because he'd been compelled to. Since I couldn't remember our second encounter, I wasn't sure if he'd felt any pleasure or not.

Dull fury took over and I wished I could reanimate Lust's corpse and kill her all over again. A smile slowly spread as I fantasized about blasting her rotting blond corpse apart. I'd shoot off her arms first, then her legs, then I'd cut her in half and watch her pieces squirm. I'd finish her off by pumping a full clip into her liquefied brain.

It was weird to be having zombie fantasies, I mused when I entered the base and backed the SUV into the garage. I'd never spent much time thinking about the undead before. Then again, I'd never spent much time thinking about shape shifters before I'd become one. Now it seemed that paranormal creatures were all I could think about.

Mark was waiting for me in the living room when I opened the door. At first I thought he was going to offer me yet another apology, but his expression was serious rather than apologetic. "Pack your suitcase," he ordered. "We're heading to New Orleans."

Well used to obeying commands without question, I sprinted for the stairs. I could move much faster now and was inside my room and gathering my clothes in seconds.

I stuffed all of my clothing into my suitcase, collected my toiletries from the bathroom and grabbed the black backpack that contained my sniper rifle and ammo from the closet. Despite my speed, I was the last one to arrive at the garage.

Flynn took my suitcase and crammed it in with the rest of the bags in the back. As always, I kept my backpack on my lap as I slid into the SUV beside Kala. I rarely let my sniper rifle out of my sight. It had cost far too much to allow anyone to steal it.

"What are we hunting this time?" I asked Kala.

"Zombies," she replied with a straight face.

Reece met my eyes in the rearview mirror when my mouth dropped open. He gave me a knowing look before returning his attention to the winding track that would take us to the security gate. He'd felt my shock and recognition and I figured he knew I was lying about being unable to sense him. This went beyond merely feeling him in my head. It almost seemed as if we'd read each other's minds.

Flynn flicked me a sideways glance when I shuddered. "Don't worry, I hate zombies, too," he said, misreading the reason for my distress.

"You've actually seen real live zombies?" I asked.

"You mean real *dead* zombies," he laughed. "Just once and it's something I'll never forget."

Kala smiled as she recalled their encounter with the walking dead. "You punched that thing so hard its head came clean off."

"I had brains and rotting flesh all over me," he said. "I could taste it in the back of my throat every time I breathed."

"I thought he was going to puke," she confided to me. "I've never seen him turn that white before."

Flynn leaned forward to glare across me at her. "You can't tell me you weren't freaked out by it."

"Of course I was freaked out," she said with a shrug. "It's not every day you see a corpse walking around." Her golden eyes turned sly as she taunted him. "At least I didn't almost throw up."

"No," Reece said and glanced in the mirror. "You were too busy trying to rip its arms off to worry about puking."

"You were just as bad," she accused. "As I recall, you did tear one of its arms off. Then you beat it into the ground with its own limb despite the fact that it was already dead by then."

Mark turned to speak to me, but his words were far from reassuring. "It's disconcerting for anyone to see a zombie for the first time, but shifters tend to react more strongly to them than humans do. I'm still not sure why." His frown indicated that he wasn't happy with his lack of knowledge when it came to our species.

"Is he serious?" I whispered to Kala.

"Yep. You'll see what he's talking about once you come face to face with one."

"Unfortunately," our boss went on, "you're all going to have to get used to them. A voodoo priestess contacted our organization and advised that she saw several zombies in one of the cemeteries in New Orleans last night. I have no idea how she knew we existed, or how she found our number." He wasn't ecstatic about the breach in security, but there was little he could do about it.

"How many zombies are we talking about?" Kala asked uneasily.

"Over a dozen," he replied. "She believes that they were just practice and that whoever is behind this will shortly begin to raise more. They haven't attacked anyone so far, but that could change at any time."

Flynn clamped his hands around his upper arms and hugged himself unhappily. "Great. It sounds like we'll soon be facing a zombie horde. Isn't it a little early for Halloween?"

It was the last week of September and there were still five weeks before the spooky holiday would commence. I'd rarely bothered to celebrate Halloween, since I'd never had friends to go trick or treating with. To be honest, the idea of ghosts and ghouls had always given me the creeps.

"How can you kill something that is technically already dead?" I asked.

"Fire is the quickest and surest way," Mark replied. "Beheading them is just as effective."

"Pumping half a dozen rounds into their heads also does the trick," Reece said without looking at me. The image of me blasting Lust's face apart returned. It was disconcerting not to know if the picture came from me or from him.

Chapter Five

We didn't head to the international airport, but instead drove to the same private strip that we'd used when Mark and I had first landed near Denver over two months ago.

"Where will we be staying in New Orleans?" I asked Kala when she sat beside me on the small jet. There was enough room for everyone to have their own row, but she preferred to sit close to me. I didn't mind the company and it would give me the opportunity to ask her questions.

"Our base in the Rocky Mountains is just one of many scattered around the country," she replied. "We'll be using a similar compound that is situated near New Orleans. It's close enough to reach the city within forty-five minutes, but not too close. There's always a chance that one of us will go on a rampage when the full moon rises again."

It had only been just over a week since I'd changed into a werewolf and I still wasn't at the stage where I could joke about my affliction. Soon, I'd be reduced to an uncontrollable beast again. It was distressing that I couldn't remember what happened during those three nights. None of us could recall what we did or what we ate during this period. Maybe it was just as well. I wasn't sure I'd want to remember chowing down on a deer and whatever other animals that I consumed.

Mark had been tasked by his superiors to keep us under control and had constructed our enclosures to keep us safely penned up. He'd arranged for all of the compounds to have another enclosure erected to contain me as well. I assumed he'd called ahead to speed up the construction of the new barrier in our base near New Orleans. There was no telling how long it would take us to hunt down the zombies and their creator and it was better to be safe than sorry.

It took almost three hours to fly from Denver to New Orleans and we landed on another private airstrip. We were carrying enough weapons to take down a small army and it made sense that we'd avoid touching down anywhere where we might be searched.

My stomach growled in complaint and Kala smirked and shot me a sideways look. Shifters burned up a lot of energy even when we were sitting still and we all had to eat frequently. There hadn't been any food on the plane and I wasn't the only one who was hungry. "Is there any chance we can stop for a meal?" she asked as we packed our gear into the back of a black SUV. It looked identical to the one that we'd left behind in Colorado. One thing I'd noticed about the PIA was that they tended to stick to the same make and model when it came to vehicles.

"We'll grab something as soon as we reach the city," Agent Steel promised. He didn't require food as often as the rest of us, but even he had to be hungry by now.

As always, Reece drove. I wasn't sure if he had severe control issues, or if it was Mark's preference for his second in charge to drive. Shifters had far better reflexes than humans. Maybe he felt safer with a werewolf behind the wheel. I sure hadn't felt safe with his driving skills at first, but I'd eventually become used to his reckless speed and aggressive techniques.

Mark punched our destination into the GPS and the SUV took off. We drove through a marshy area that quickly became a smelly swamp. It only took half an hour to reach the outskirts of New Orleans. I peered through the windows as we drove into the heart of the town. Hurricane Katrina had devastated much of the city years ago. Some of the population had fled with no intention of ever returning. Despite the threat that yet another natural disaster could strike during hurricane season, the city was still a popular tourist destination for much of the year.

We parked outside the restaurant that Mark had chosen and filed inside. It was well past the lunchtime rush and only a few people were sitting at the tables. The menu was in both English and French. The restaurant was small and cozy and we dragged two tables together so we could remain in a group. I sat as far from Reece as I could get. I still wasn't used to the idea that we were bonded and that we now shared a psychic link. We'd reached a mutual decision to keep our distance without saying so out loud.

We ordered our meals and I chose a burger and fries. Kala had the same, but ordered her meat rare. I couldn't bring myself to eat meat if it was still bleeding. I almost gagged when I thought about what I ate while I was in wolf form. For all I knew, I'd been snacking on diseased rats.

Seeing me turn an alarming shade of green and guessing the reason why, Flynn nudged me with his elbow. "Try not to think about it," he told me, accurately reading my expression. "It took me months to get used to the idea that I'd eat anything with a heartbeat. This one time, I woke up near the remains of what I think was a cat and puked for a whole hour."

Horrified by the mental picture that his confession had conjured, I bolted out of my chair and darted into the ladies room. I bent over the sink, but my stomach was empty and I could only manage a dry heave. He might have been trying to help me, but he'd had the opposite effect.

The toilet behind me flushed and a woman with dark skin and hair in a multitude of braids looked at me in concern when she stepped out of the cubicle. "Are you all right, child?" Her accent was foreign and musical. Her dress was colorful and had elephants, giraffes and other African animals on it. It was easy to guess her heritage.

Turning on the tap, I nodded and splashed water on my face. "I'm okay. My stomach is just a bit upset." Picturing yourself devouring a cat would do it every time.

Handing me a paper towel, the woman froze when she met my eyes. Whatever she saw in them frightened her badly. Backing away slowly, she hit the wall, then turned and fled, looking over her shoulder to make sure I wasn't following her.

"That was weird," I said to my reflection as I dried my face and hands.

Feeling much better, I took my seat and waved away the concern from my team before they could bombard me with questions. "I'm fine. Did anyone see that lady who ran out of the bathroom?"

"I did," Reece replied without looking up. "Something scared her off."

"I'm pretty sure it was me," I said glumly.

Mark glanced around to make sure no one was close enough to overhear us. "What did you do?" he asked in a low voice that wouldn't carry.

"Nothing," I replied with a shrug. "I was washing my hands and she gave me a paper towel, then looked into my eyes and freaked out."

He mused about the problem and waited for the waitress to deliver our meals before speaking. "It's possible that she's a voodoo priestess, or maybe even a Wiccan," he said. "They sometimes have the ability to sense beings that aren't human."

"Oh." Picking up a French fry, I bit into it to see if my stomach would rebel. It didn't and I swallowed the food down. "Why did she run away from me?"

"Because we're monsters," Kala reminded me around a mouthful of food.

Mark sent her a withering stare. "The only thing that's monstrous at this table is your manners."

Sending our boss a sunny grin that showed chunks of meat stuck in her teeth, Kala took another gigantic bite of her bloody burger. "You love me," she said around the half-chewed food.

"Yes," he agreed. "But at times like these I seriously wonder why."

Amused by their banter, I bit into my well-cooked burger and kept thoughts of raw, bloody meat firmly out of my mind. Reece watched me from the corner of his eye and I hated the fact that he knew what I was feeling. A flare of remorse came from him, then he clamped down on his feelings so hard that I could barely sense him at all. If he could accomplish that, then so could I and I resolved to try to get a handle on my emotions.

"What's the plan, boss?" Flynn asked when we'd finished our meals and the table had been cleared. We were drinking sodas to give us an excuse to linger for a bit longer.

"We need to question the voodoo priestess who made the call to our organization," Mark said. "Her store is in the French Quarter." It wasn't a surprise that the PIA had tracked her down. They probably had the technology to find anyone on the planet.

We drove a short distance and found a spot on a narrow street. I'd never been to New Orleans before and the French Quarter was a riot of color and ethnicities. Most of the buildings on this street were two or three stories high. Most had balconies clinging to the walls. Others had galleries supported by columns and an abundance of flowering plants to brighten the view even more. It was very different from the far more modern buildings and skyscrapers I was used to seeing in larger cities.

People watched us suspiciously as we stood in a cluster on the sidewalk. We were clearly visitors to the city and we obviously weren't tourists. With his coffee colored skin, only Flynn would have been able to fit into this neighborhood without notice. Even his green eyes weren't an anomaly among this particular mixture of races.

Mark surveyed the street and pointed at a store that sold voodoo paraphernalia. It was wedged between a clothing boutique and a bar. "Reece and Kala, wait out here," he instructed. They acknowledged him with a nod while Flynn and I followed him inside.

A bell jingled when Mark pushed the door open. I could see why he didn't want all of us to enter the store. It was crammed with goods that I had no hope of being able to identify. There was barely enough room for the three of us to walk between the narrow shelves. They were stacked high with what appeared to be ingredients. For what, I didn't want to know.

I'd read books about voodoo witchcraft and had had no inkling that any of it might actually be real. If zombies existed, then it was possible that curses might work as well. Getting on the wrong side of a voodoo practitioner was probably a very bad idea.

It was dark at the back of the store. A woman stood behind the counter, almost hidden in the shadows. Without my heightened eyesight, it would have been difficult to see her. It took Mark a few seconds to spot her and he strode over to the counter. Her dark skin was wrinkled and her eyes were aged and weary. She was somewhere in her seventies or eighties. Her pure white hair had been wound on the top of her head in a towering pile of braids. Her dress was almost as colorful as the woman's from the restaurant.

She stared at my boss impassively when he approached her. "I guess I know a cop when I see one," she rasped in a voice that spoke of long years of cigarette smoking. Her accent was musical and foreign.

"We're federal agents," he corrected her and flashed his ID. "I understand that you called the organization that we belong to last night. Can you tell us any more about the zombies you saw?"

Switching her attention to Flynn and me, she smiled craftily. "You'll have to hunt down their master, the Zombie King," she said. "It was a good idea to bring shifters with you. Everyone knows they hate the undead more than anything else on this planet."

"I didn't realize that was common knowledge," Flynn said with a cheeky wink.

Cackling out a laugh, it turned into a cough and she had to stop to catch her breath. "Most of those who are aware of the dark underworld know that shape shifters and the undead are mortal enemies." She shifted her gaze back to Mark. "I hope you brought along weapons that can kill the reanimated."

"We were planning on using fire to eradicate them," he replied.

"That'll do it, but the Zombie King won't like it if you burn his puppets," the voodoo priestess warned him.

"Do you know who he is?" I asked.

Examining me for a long second, the priestess motioned me closer. "You two can leave," she said, dismissing the men with a wave of her gnarled, arthritic hand. "I want to talk to the girl alone."

Unhappy with her order, Mark was about to protest, but I turned to him and put my hand on his arm. My grip was far stronger than any normal teen's. It was a reminder that I wouldn't be in any physical danger. "I'll be fine."

Flynn wasn't happy about leaving me alone either, but our boss gave him a light push that set him in motion towards the door.

Turning back to the priestess, I was alarmed to see that she'd rounded the counter and was now standing only a few inches away from me. She'd moved so quickly and quietly that I hadn't even heard her. My new senses should have been sharp enough to detect any movement. Maybe the voodoo practitioner had powers I wasn't even aware of.

"You are new to being a werewolf," she said wisely.

"Yes. I only turned a week ago."

"May I see your scar?"

I hesitated at the odd request. "Which one?" I asked.

"The one on your right shoulder, child."

Amazed and disturbed that she knew about my old scar, I shrugged out of my jacket and pulled the strap of my white tank top aside. The priestess leaned forward to see the mangled bite mark that had been left by a dog so long ago. She shifted her attention to my left shoulder and moved the strap aside so she could study the second mark. "I thought I sensed turmoil within your spirit," she said in a low murmur.

"What turmoil?" I asked as I put my jacket back on.

"You have been bitten by two paranormal beings. They are natural enemies and now your spirit is being torn between two opposing forces."

I'd never heard of dogs and werewolves being natural enemies before, but I was still pretty new to the whole paranormal world. As far as I knew, ordinary dogs weren't magical and her theory didn't make much sense. "I'm sure my spirit is fine," I said and tried to steer her back to the reason why I was there. "Do you know who the Zombie King is and where we can find him?"

"I do not," the priestess replied and slowly made her way back behind the counter. "I only know that he is new to New Orleans." She pronounced the name of the city in a way that made it sound exotic. "He is a young bokor who is just beginning to harness his dark powers." She met my eyes and hers were frightened. "You must stop him before he raises the wrong zombie."

"What will happen if he does?" I wasn't even sure what she meant by that. Weren't all zombies the same? A shiver worked its way down my spine in anticipation of her answer.

"Chaos," she said succinctly. "Once he loses control, the undead will immediately seek out food and everyone in this city will be in danger."

I didn't really want to know what zombies ate, but countless horror movies all said the same thing. They'd eat either human flesh, brains, or possibly both. If we didn't find the Zombie King and put him down, the citizens of New Orleans would soon become snacks for the walking dead.

Chapter Six

"What did the priestess say?" Kala asked as soon as I stepped out onto the street.

My face must have been pale, because she touched my arm in concern. "She said the Zombie King is new to the city," I told her with the others listening in intently. "He's a bokor, whatever that means. He is also apparently new to zombie raising. She thinks he's going to raise the wrong type of zombie or something and lose control. If he does, his pet corpses will start chowing down on humans."

Mark hadn't known me for very long, but he could still tell that I was hiding something from him. "What else did she say?" he prompted.

Knowing I couldn't evade his question, I shoved my hands into my front pockets. "She knew I was new to being a shifter and she wanted to see my scar. That's all." No way was I going to tell them the rest of what she'd told me. Her theory about my tortured spirit was the kind of crazy talk that could get a person locked up.

"Did she know where we can find this guy?" Flynn asked.

I shook my head. "That's all she could tell me."

"I should have known it was a bokor," Agent Steel said almost to himself.

"What exactly is a bokor?" I asked. Apart from reading a couple of fiction novels, I knew very little about voodoo. It wasn't a topic that had been taught in any of the high schools that I'd attended.

Reece answered my question. "A bokor is someone who studies the dark voodoo arts. They can raise the dead and can cast harmful curses and spells. It's not a good idea to get on their bad side." His thought echoed the one I'd had earlier almost too eerily.

"Garrett wants to be Mark when he grows up," Flynn said solemnly. "He actually reads the research that the boss assigns to us."

Kala snorted a laugh, then sobered when Mark flicked them both a warning look.

"Where to now?" Reece asked as we piled back into the SUV.

"I want to examine the cemetery where the priestess saw the zombies," Mark replied and called up the address on the GPS. "We need to see how many corpses he's managed to raise now."

Again, we only had a short drive to reach our destination. I'd heard about the cemeteries in New Orleans and this one lived up to its reputation. They were known as 'Cities of the Dead' and it was easy to see why. Row upon row of ancient crypts and mausoleums stretched out far and wide. The crypts were a mixture of white marble and dark gray stone. All were aged and weathered. The city had been mostly built on a swamp, hence the aboveground graves.

Even before we climbed out of the car, I sensed that something was wrong. A cold, scaly finger seemed to scrape down the back of my neck. I had to force myself to follow the others through the gates. A few tourists were scattered around the cemetery, taking photos and reading the worn inscriptions. It was easily the oldest graveyard that I'd ever been to. It was also by far the creepiest.

"All of these graves are really, really old," I said, trying not to let my teeth chatter. It was a warm, humid day, but I felt cold all the same. "Surely the bodies would just be bones and dust by now. How dangerous can walking skeletons possibly be?"

Mark continued down the row, checking each crypt and mausoleum for signs of disturbances. "A talented bokor can reanimate a corpse well enough to make them seem almost alive," he explained as he searched.

"How?" I asked. I now had to consciously will my legs to move. The closer we drew to the heart of the cemetery, the less I wanted to be there. No one else seemed to be affected by the wrongness that apparently only I could feel.

"By using spells that involve blood, usually," he replied. "Either animal or human blood. Human blood is more powerful, of course. I once saw a zombie that was so lifelike it was almost impossible to tell that he was really dead."

"How did you know he was a zombie?"

"He wasn't breathing," he said with a wry smile. His gaze sharpened when he saw that my arms were wrapped around my torso and I was holding myself tightly. "What's wrong?"

Was he kidding? There was an aura of evil coming from the crypts that was so thick I could almost taste it. "Can't you feel that?" I asked and received three confused stares.

"Feel what?" Kala asked.

"Evil," Reece said, no doubt stealing the emotions directly from me. He'd been the only one not to stare at me in confusion. He pointed at the closest crypt. "It's coming from there."

To me, it seemed to be coming from everywhere, but it did appear to be stronger near the elaborately decorated grave. A marble angel stared down at us with a melancholy expression as we moved to surround the crypt. Kala put her hand around my waist to offer me comfort.

"Keep watch to make sure no one approaches," Mark ordered us and I did my best to comply.

Reece searched for signs that the grave had been disturbed. Hunkering down, he touched some flakes that had been chipped off the marble. "It's been opened recently," he deduced and stood. That would account for the faint hint of spoiled meat in the air.

Kala and I kept our eyes on the tourists to make sure none of them was about to wander in our direction. Reece and Flynn worked together to slide the top of the crypt aside. They made it look easy, but the marble had to be heavy. Mark stepped forward to look down into the crypt. "Ladies and gentlemen, we have confirmation of zombies," he pronounced. He took his cell phone out and snapped a shot of the occupant.

Flynn looked down into the grave and hatred flashed over his face. Kala took a step forward and it was my turn to hold onto her. Her body was quivering slightly in suppressed rage. Reece took a quick glance into the grave and I felt anticipation of bloodshed coming from him. His expression gave nothing of his battle lust away.

Kala took hold of herself and propelled me forward so I could take my first look at a reanimated corpse. Bracing myself and trying to ignore the sense of evil, I grudgingly looked down into the dark opening. The Zombie King wasn't as powerful as I'd imagined because his zombie looked far from fresh. Rotting meat was barely held together over exposed bone and sinews.

I froze when the undead creature turned its head with a creaking sound like a rusty door slowly being pushed ajar. Its eyes opened and twin milky orbs glared up at me. It hissed in warning, revealing its few remaining teeth and a bloated, moss covered tongue. Even worse than that hideous sight was the sense of alien thoughts that invaded my head. It was sluggish, maybe because it was daylight. I had the feeling that if darkness had held sway, it would have gone for my throat.

The next thing I knew I was sprinting for my life. Someone was calling my name, but I was too panicked to listen. A hand caught my arm and yanked me to a halt. Only when he turned me around and pulled me to him did I realize that it was Reece.

I was so distraught by my first encounter with a zombie that I let myself sink into him when he pulled me in close. His hand ran up and down my back soothingly until my trembling finally stopped. His thoughts were calming, but I knew he was confused by my reaction. Instead of feeling rage and the need to destroy the thing, I'd been terrified almost to tears. He didn't know that he wasn't the only one who could get inside my mind. I knew why we could touch each other's thoughts, but I couldn't explain why I could sense the zombie.

Pushing away from him, I was ashamed not just by my reaction to the zombie, but to him as well. He caught my chin in his hand and forced me to look into his eyes. "Don't be embarrassed. We all have a strong reaction the first time we see a zombie."

To be honest, my horror and fright had fled quickly once his arms had come around me. I had to dredge up the image of the hissing corpse to remember why I'd run in the first place. He had the ability to wipe away my distress with one touch, which didn't make me happy at all. Being bonded to him was going to be even harder to deal with than I'd thought.

Footsteps approached and I moved away from him just as Kala jogged over to us. "Are you okay?" she asked.

Nodding, I smiled sheepishly. "I don't know what came over me. The zombie looked at me with its horrible white eyes, hissed at me and my mind went completely blank." Well, not completely blank. I'd felt a craving for human flesh and blood that hadn't come from either me, or from my inner beast. The need to feed had come from the bundle of rotting meat and bones lying in the crypt.

Mark and Flynn were right behind her and they overheard my explanation. "We have a couple of things to take care of, then we'll head to our base where we can discuss this in private," Agent Steel said. I'd been seen bolting away from the cemetery and people watched us suspiciously from doorways and windows up and down the street. "Kala, stay with Lexi. Reece, Flynn, you're with me."

Kala and I made our way back to the SUV while the guys headed to the cemetery. I was surprised to see how far I'd run in such a short space of time. It was no wonder people were staring. I must have been moving far faster than was normal for a human.

"What now?" I asked when we reached the SUV.

"We found signs of blood on thirty or so graves," she explained. "We also found a circle on the ground that had been drawn in blood. The bokor scrubbed most of it away to hide his ritual, but now that the zombies have risen, he can call them forth without going through the full ritual again. He just needs to sprinkle some fresh blood on the circle to activate it. The guys are setting up motion sensing cameras near the graves that have been marked with blood. The cameras will tell us when they rise so we don't waste time sitting around in the cemetery."

It was a good idea and I was grateful I wouldn't have to spend more time than was necessary in the graveyard. We needed to head to the base to gear up before we could face these things again. I was glad that I'd have a reprieve before we had to return.

Chapter Seven

It took the guys a quarter of an hour to set up the cameras and to return to the SUV. A pungent smell filled the vehicle as we drove through more swamp land. After a forty-five minute journey, we ended up in dense, marshy woods.

While the trees were different from the ones in the compound in the Rocky Mountains, the fence was the same. Thirty feet high, both it and the gate were topped with razor wire. They provided an effective deterrent to keep any trespassers out. The barrier had the added security of being electrified.

Our trek through the woods was short and I was amazed to see a familiar two story concrete building ahead. It was an exact replica of the compound in

Colorado. It seemed that the PIA stuck to the same template with their buildings as well as with their cars.

We backed into the garage then we climbed out of the SUV and entered the same long hallway I was used to seeing in our usual home. Mark placed his hand on the scanner to open the door to the main area. "You'll have to scan your prints on the computer before I can give you access to the doors," he said over his shoulder as he pushed the door open.

I thought all of the compounds would be linked together through the computer system, but it seemed that I was wrong. The main room was exactly the same as the base in Colorado, except for the furniture. The dining table, chairs and coffee table were white. The bright yellow rug on the floor in the living room clashed badly with the brown leather couches.

The guys were probably happy that they still had gym equipment and a boxing ring to keep them fit and occupied. I just hoped there was a gun range so I could practice my skills.

We took the winding staircase up to the second floor and entered the communications room. It was identical to the other one down to the black leather L-shaped couch. Mark lined us up and we took turns placing our right hands on the computer table. Once our prints had been recorded, we returned to the ground floor again.

"I need coffee before you launch into your plan," Kala said.

"I second that motion," Flynn agreed. Out of the four shifters in the squad, he was the calmest in temperament. Snakes were usually fairly placid until they were provoked into an attack. Our blond companion on the other hand, was playful and affectionate, just like the cat she changed into. She could also be vicious when she was angry. So far, she hadn't turned her anger on any of us and it seemed to be reserved for the bad guys. Reece was similar to me. We both tended to need time alone and were a little distant from the others. We were part of the same team, yet we didn't quite feel as though we belonged. Or at least that was how it seemed to me.

We all wanted liquid refreshment, so I assisted in the kitchen. Kala couldn't cook to save her life, but she was excellent at making coffee. An unknown person had stocked the fridge and cupboards for us. I put cookies on a plate in case anyone wanted a snack. My stomach was still unsettled from my first zombie sighting, so I stuck to coffee when we sat down on the couch. I could now gulp down my beverage while it was still hot, but chose to sip it slowly.

Mark picked up his coffee, decided it was too hot and put it down again. If I didn't know better, I'd say he was procrastinating. When he finally looked up, I saw that he was concerned. "What's wrong?" I asked. Somehow, I knew that whatever was bothering him had something to do with me.

"When did you first sense the zombies?" he asked.

"I felt a sense of wrongness when we were about a block away from the cemetery," I replied with a grimace at the memory of the spectral finger on the back of my neck. "The closer we drew to it, the stronger the sense of evil became."

Kala looked at each of the men then huffed out a sigh. "Since none of them are brave enough to say it, I will." She turned to me squarely. "You shouldn't be able to sense them. They shouldn't be able to sense you. Like vampires, they're usually unable to function during the day, yet it woke up and hissed at you. That isn't normal."

While I appreciated her candor, I was shaken by her pronouncement. "What does this mean? Is there something wrong with me?" I was glad that I hadn't mentioned that I'd felt it in my head. What would they do if they knew that I could pick up its thoughts? Would they turn me away, or possibly even lock me up? They'd never encountered something like me before and the thought terrified me.

Mark shifted uncomfortably on his seat. "I believe it has something to do with whatever else the voodoo priestess said to you. The part you haven't told us about yet," he added pointedly.

Kala had been right when she said there were no secrets in the Shifter Squad. I was going to have to come clean with them. "She said I've been bitten by two unnatural beings and that my spirit is now at war," I said with great reluctance. Reece's shoulders hunched at being called unnatural and I immediately wished I could take the words back.

Mark picked up a cookie, but he only toyed with it rather than taking a bite. "That sounds dire."

"It also sounds crazy," I said. "I wasn't bitten by anything supernatural when I was a baby. It was just a normal dog. You can call my Dad and ask him about it if you like," I said in exasperation when they all stared at me doubtfully. "How can a dog bite from so long ago possibly be having an adverse effect on me now?"

Biting into his cookie, Mark chewed slowly and avoided my gaze as he took his time to wash it down with coffee. "Despite what Philip told you," he finally said, "I'm not convinced that it was a dog that bit you. Whatever it really was that left that scar, the zombie seemed to react to it." This wasn't the first time he'd told me he thought that something other than a canine had bitten me, but he wasn't any more forthcoming about the old scar on my right shoulder.

"Great, I guess I'm now a zombie detector," I said wearily.

Flynn didn't see that as a bad thing and sat forward excitedly. "This could actually work in our favor."

"How?" Reece asked. He was masking his emotions, but I felt a trickle of concern for me and felt warmed by it. I reminded myself that the bond was to blame for any changes he might be feeling towards me. I dredged up his speech about how I wasn't his type and that he didn't want me. The warmth evaporated, leaving me feeling bereft and alone.

"If Lexi can sense them at a distance, then she can lead us right to them," Flynn replied. "We won't have to search every grave, crypt and mausoleum in town one by one. We won't even have to search every cemetery in town to find them."

"He has a good point," Mark said. "I hadn't thought of that."

"I'm more than just a pretty face, you know," Flynn said with a grin.

His amusement was infectious and I couldn't help but smile. A short yet strong sense of jealousy came from Reece and immediately quenched my grin. He picked up his mug, took a long swallow and avoided looking in my direction. I wasn't an expert on bonding between werewolves, but this seemed like a bad sign. While I'd already been hopelessly attracted to him, he'd been indifferent to me before he'd been bamboozled by Lust. I'd had a crush on him from almost the first moment that we'd met, but the last thing I'd wanted was for us to be forced together by paranormal means. His jealousy could only be caused by our mystical link.

"Here's the plan," Mark said, snapping my attention back to him and thankfully diverting me from my inner turmoil. "We'll wait until the cameras alert us that the zombies have risen, then we'll move in and turn them to ash."

I'd never burned anything to death before and I was frightened that I'd accidentally set myself, or one of the others, on fire. "What kind of weapons are we going to use?" I hoped it was something more advanced than lighting sticks on fire and waving them around like an angry mob from the middle-ages.

"Modified flamethrowers," Kala responded. "Don't worry, you won't have any trouble using them," she reassured me when she saw my unease.

"What do we do if the bokor turns up while we're frying his minions?" Flynn asked. "He hasn't caused anyone any harm so far, that we know of. Are we going to kill him, or just incapacitate him?"

"Incapacitate," Mark responded. "We'll take him into custody and call the Containment Squad in to retrieve him."

"We have a Containment Squad?" I asked. I was still sadly ignorant about the PIA. Few knew that the Paranormal Investigation Agency even existed. It was a clandestine organization that had been created to deal with the things that went bump in the night. Sadly, I was now one of the creatures that they normally did their best to eradicate.

"We sure do," Kala said. "We might be the Track and Kill Squad, but we don't always kill everything we hunt down."

"We only kill the ones that have harmed or slaughtered humans," Flynn explained.

"So, we'll slap some handcuffs on the Zombie King and he'll go to prison?" It seemed like an anticlimactic end for someone who had the power to raise corpses and force them to do his bidding.

Mark finished off his cookie before responding to my question. "It's a special prison and the inmates will never have a chance of parole or escape."

"I hope it's more secure than the place where the seven psychics were held," I said dourly.

"It is," he replied firmly. "There has never been a successful escape from the PIA prison in the past hundred and fifty years."

I was flabbergasted by that nugget of information. "The agency has been around for that long?"

He nodded, picked up his mug and slouched back against the couch. "That was when it officially became an organization, although it had a different name back then. I'll give you access to the archives, if you're interested in learning more about the PIA." He sent a reproachful look at Kala and Flynn, neither of whom were even slightly interested in learning about the history of the agency.

"That'd be great," I replied sincerely. The research would be fascinating, I had no doubt.

Finishing her coffee, Kala stood and beckoned for me to follow her. "Let's get some practice in before we head out later tonight."

My mug was still half full, so I took it with me. We entered the long hallway and turned left. She stopped halfway down the hall and put her hand on the scanner next to a door I'd never been inside before. I had a moment of disorientation when I remembered we were no longer in Colorado. It was going to take some getting used to being in a nearly identical facility to the place I'd almost come to think of as home, yet being so far away from the Rocky Mountains.

The door unlocked and Kala pushed it open. She stepped aside and allowed me to enter first. Like the indoor gun range further down the hall, this room was long, narrow and had five lanes for target practice. Humanoid targets hung from overhead tracks that ran the length of the room, but they were made of metal rather than paper. Several different types of flamethrowers were mounted on a wall. She reached up, took one down and handed it to me. It looked like a rifle, but shot flames rather than bullets.

A long row of metal cabinets with numerous doors sat below the flamethrowers. Kala opened a door and took out a small, red, rectangular plastic canister with a hose coming out from the top. "Plug the hose into the flamethrower, attach the canister to the hook, flick the safety off and you're good to go," she said.

I took the canister and it was full of liquid. The smell told me it was a mixture of gasoline and something else that was most likely highly flammable. Following her instructions, I attached the hose then threaded a small metal ring in the top of the canister through a hook in the butt of the gun to hold it stable. I flicked the safety switch on the side of the weapon off and turned to aim at the closest target.

Fire spurted in a twenty foot arc when I pulled the trigger. "Holy crap!" I exclaimed and took my finger off the trigger. If anything flammable had been in the area, I'd have turned it to ash. Luckily, the floor, walls and ceiling were bare concrete and Kala was standing safely behind me.

"Fun, right?" she said with a grin. "Just make sure you don't accidentally point it at one of us before pulling the trigger."

Shifters could withstand heat, but I doubted we were invulnerable to an open flame. "I'd better get some more practice in," I decided. Shooting bullets was easy, you just had to aim and pull the trigger. Flames were unpredictable and a strong wind could easily create havoc.

I found it far easier to bathe the target in flames when I moved to within ten feet of it. I circled the metal man, sending short bursts of fire at it until I was confident that I wouldn't torch one of my team mates by accident.

Kala took down one of the flamethrowers and kept me company until the door opened and the guys filed in. My canister was empty and the gun had grown uncomfortably warm by then. I put the flamethrower down on the floor and stood near the back wall while all three men took practice shots at the targets. My gaze returned again and again to Reece. He moved with lithe grace and something tightened deep inside me. His eyes flicked to my face and I was mortified to realize that he was picking up on my traitorous feelings of desire.

"I need coffee," I murmured to Kala and left the room.

She was right on my heels and followed me into the kitchen. "Getting a bit hot in there?" she teased, waving a hand at my face to cool me down.

I turned crimson as I switched the coffee machine on. "Do you realize how embarrassing it is to have feelings for someone and to know with utter certainty that they don't reciprocate them at all?" I asked her in something close to despair.

Her grin disappeared and an intent expression replaced it. "How do you know he doesn't feel the same way about you?"

I hated to admit it, but the words tumbled out anyway. "Because I can feel it! I might be eighteen now, but he still thinks of me as a child. The only thing he feels for me is guilt for turning me into one of you."

She mulled over my confession. "Are you saying that you know what Garrett is thinking and feeling? You can sense him the same way that he can sense you?"

I nodded miserably and poured coffee into two mugs. "I lied to Mark. I don't know why. I guess I just didn't want to admit that we really are bonded."

Pouring cream into her coffee, she handed the bottle to me and stirred in sugar. "Is being bonded such a bad thing?"

"Of course it is!" I couldn't believe she even had to ask me that. "Would you want to be psychically linked to someone who doesn't even want you around? To know he knows everything you're thinking and feeling and that he feels pity for you?"

She put her hand on my shoulder and I almost broke into tears. "I'm sorry, Lexi." Her compassion was genuine. "I didn't know it was like that."

"Don't say anything to Mark, okay?" It was bad enough that I'd blabbed to her. I didn't want everyone else to feel sorry for me as well.

"I won't," she promised, then linked her arm through mine and urged me into the living room. We sat down on the couch and drank our coffee in silence. Neither of us wanted to watch TV. We had a long wait ahead for darkness to fall and for the hunt to begin.

Chapter Eight

Flynn cooked fish for dinner and Mark made a salad. I wasn't hungry for a change and I was too tense to even think about eating. No one else seemed to have the same problem as me. When they sat down to eat at the dining table, I excused myself and withdrew to my bedroom up on the second level.

We'd chosen the same rooms that we used in Colorado out of habit. My door was the third one on the right. I'd only been inside long enough to dump my suitcase and sniper rifle just inside the door. I now had a chance to examine the room in further detail. The bed was queen-size, just like the last one, but it was blond wood instead of white. So were the twin bedside tables. I didn't have an elegant dresser with a

73

mirror and stool this time. I'd rarely used it anyway and wouldn't miss it much.

A chest of drawers the same color as the rest of the furniture had been placed to the right of the bed where the dresser had been in my old bedroom. Most of my clothes went into it and I hung my jackets in the closet. I stashed my backpack with the sniper rifle in the closet as well where it would be out of sight, but easy to retrieve.

Finished unpacking, I moved into the bathroom. It was identical to my previous bathroom, which made things easier. I unpacked my toiletries, then glanced at my pale face in the mirror. My eyes were wide and frightened at the prospect of facing thirty or so zombies. It had been bad enough seeing a single corpse lying there in its tomb. I wasn't looking forward to seeing a whole bunch of them up and shambling about. I dreaded how awful it would be to have them inside my mind.

With fire as our main weapon, I thought it would be safest to tie my hair up into a ponytail. It made me look about fifteen, but that couldn't be helped. I changed out of my white t-shirt and jeans, swapping the outfit for something more appropriate for zombie hunting. I chose a black t-shirt and khaki colored cargo pants. I didn't bother with a jacket. It was doubtful I'd get cold enough to need one and my scars were hidden by the shirt. I decided to leave my holster behind and to carry my gun and ammo in my pockets instead. Thanks to my newly enhanced strength, I could carry a lot more gear now.

My pockets bulged by the time I was done stocking up. The window behind the bed was covered by a curtain this time. I shifted the gauzy material aside and glanced outside to see that the sun had set. All of the windows were heavily tinted so no one could see inside. They'd need a ladder to be able to climb up high enough to peer in anyway.

I left my room and Mark met me in the coms room when I emerged from the hallway. "You have excellent timing," he said and nodded towards one of the monitors that were mounted on the wall above the computer table. The cameras in the cemetery had come to life as soon as the zombies had begun to rise.

I watched as a heavy marble lid was shifted aside and a skeletal arm emerged from the crypt. My nose wrinkled in disgust as the creature wormed its way out through the narrow opening and fell onto its face. Slowly and ponderously, it managed to stand. Several other zombies had already escaped from their confines. They stood there motionlessly, staring at nothing as far as I could tell.

"What are they doing?" I asked.

"They're waiting for their master. It appears that he commanded them to rise automatically once the sun goes down."

"We'd better get back to New Orleans before they start carrying off virgins to snack on," Flynn called from the bottom of the stairs. He'd raised his voice for Mark's benefit rather than for mine. I'd have been able to hear him if he'd whispered.

"Zombies prefer virgins?" I asked skeptically. I'd never heard that one before. If it was true, then I was glad I no longer fell into that category.

"He's joking," Kala said as I descended to the ground floor. She handed me a spare flamethrower that she'd kindly already assembled. I checked the safety to make sure it was on.

"Hey, the bokor could be using his undead puppets to collect virgins," Flynn said in self-defense. "We don't know what his plan is yet."

"It's time for us to find out," Mark said before the pair could start squabbling in earnest.

We fell in and followed him into the hallway and then to the garage. Reece was loading extra flamethrowers and spare canisters of fuel into the back of the SUV. We had enough firepower to set the entire cemetery on fire if we needed to.

Driving quickly, it only took us half an hour to reach the outskirts of the city this time. Reece had to slow down once we hit traffic and I felt his impatience. Unlike me, he was eager to get this over and done with. While he instinctively hated the undead and felt compelled to destroy them, he was able to master his emotions. I didn't have his self-control and I was nearly gibbering in fear when we pulled up around the corner from the cemetery.

Mark took a small black device that looked like a cell phone out of his pocket. He keyed something into it then climbed out.

"What did he just do?" I asked Flynn as we stuck to the shadows and headed towards the graveyard. We weren't exactly inconspicuous as we scurried along carrying our bulky weapons.

"He shut off the CCTV cameras that are watching the cemetery so no one will catch us in the act."

"Oh." It was a precaution that I never would have thought of and I was glad no one was relying on me for leadership. We were about to unleash fire in the middle of the city and someone was bound to call the cops if we were spotted. I wasn't sure if we'd be able to get the job done before the police and fire trucks arrived. Most sane people wouldn't believe that zombies existed and it would be hard to explain what we were doing. The PIA worked in the shadows and behind the scenes so civilians could go on believing that all was right with the world. If they knew that monsters truly existed no one would ever leave their homes.

We reached the fence and followed it to the gate. The cold, scaly finger was working its way down my neck to my spine again and I was breathing too fast. I could feel the zombies long before I saw them. An unnatural green haze had permeated the boneyard. Visibility was murky and the atmosphere was spooky.

As the team had already determined from their inspection of the graves, there were far more than the initial dozen zombies now. Just over thirty walking corpses were clumped together in the middle of the cemetery. Not all of the bokor's minions had been able to escape from their graves. Scrabbling sounds came from inside a few of the mausoleums. They'd been constructed so well that nothing could get in or out without a wrecking ball.

The bokor still hadn't shown up yet and I wondered what would happen if their master died before he could issue new orders. Then I remembered what the voodoo priestess had told me. They'd go in search of food and they wouldn't stop eating until someone hunted them down and ended their unnatural lives.

While their bones had survived their long decades of burial, the reanimated skeletons' clothing had long since rotted away. The Zombie King hadn't put much effort into fleshing out his small group of walking dead. Black and green flesh barely clung to bones that had turned a sickly shade of ivory with age.

I swallowed back the urge to vomit when a chunk of meat fell from one of the zombies. The stench of decay thickened and became overpowering when it splattered to the ground. I felt for Flynn when he made a gagging sound. While most shifters used their noses to detect their prey, he was different. As a wereconstrictor, his sense of taste was far more powerful than ours. With each breath that he took, it would taste as though he was swallowing down rotten meat. He might enjoy the sensation when he was transformed into his snake form, but as a human, it was disgusting.

Spreading out, we moved in to surround the undead. When I was within twenty feet of the group, they turned and hissed at me. It was good to know the range that they could sense me from, but now I was paralyzed with fear. I felt a niggling sensation in the back of my head, then the sluggish and inarticulate thoughts of the walking corpses were bombarding me. The only goal in their decayed brains was to eat and we were a walking banquet. They'd been told to stand still and to wait for their master, but the lure of food was almost enough to make them break free from their mental bondage.

"Take them down!" Mark ordered and bright orange flames lit up the night.

Reacting to the command, my hands worked automatically to flick off the safety and to pull the trigger. Shrieking shrilly in agony, the undead mob shied away from the heat but they had nowhere to run. Completely surrounded, they moved into a tight pack, which made it easier for us to annihilate them.

Once the crispy corpses stopped twitching and the buzzing in my head lessened, my fear of them began to fade. Ash, bone and the smell of seared flesh were all that remained of our targets. Some were still trapped in their graves, but they couldn't get out and we were in no danger from them.

We listened for sirens for a couple of minutes, but none sounded. We were deep in the heart of the cemetery and it seemed that our hunt had gone unnoticed. It was all too obvious that a large number of bodies had been burned. Come daylight, either locals or tourists would discover the mess and the cops would be notified.

One step ahead of me, Mark took out his cell phone and called the local Cleanup Crew. We didn't stick around to watch the cleaning process, but we did take the time to replace the dislodged crypt lids before leaving. I had no trouble sliding the heavy marble and stone back into place. Mark didn't even try to assist us. As a human, he lacked the advantage of our uncanny strength.

We'd nearly reached the SUV when Reece stopped abruptly. He turned in a circle, searching for something unseen. He was on high alert and his eyes probed the shadows. Thanks to my enhanced sight, I could easily make out objects that would be indistinct to a human. I saw no one hiding in the darkness and relaxed at the same time as he came to the conclusion that we were alone.

"What is it?" Mark asked.

"Someone was watching us," Reece said. He had his Colt in his hand and I hadn't even seen him draw it. "Whoever it was is gone now. I can hear a car driving away."

I heard it, too, but couldn't quite pinpoint which direction it was coming from.

"It had to be the bokor," Kala said. Our target might be young, but he was smart enough to watch us from a distance to see what our plan was. He now knew that we were his adversaries.

"If the voodoo priestess is right, then he's not going to be happy that we've fried his minions," Flynn deduced. "There's something like fifteen cemeteries in New Orleans, which means he has plenty more undead to choose from. I bet he's going to step up his game now that he knows we're on to him."

"Then we'd better track him down and stop him before he does anything stupid," Mark said. "Spread out and see if you can pick up his scent. Lexi, you're with me."

Still fairly new to being an agent, I didn't question his order. Carrying our flamethrowers as inconspicuously as possible, we combed the area. The only scents I picked up were hours old and there was no way to distinguish if they'd belonged to our quarry or not. I'd learned that the squad had managed to track the Seven Deadly Sinners' scent from clothing they'd left behind when they'd escaped from their prison.

We met back at the SUV after twenty minutes of scouring the streets. Flynn had some good news. "I picked up a fresh scent which disappeared only a couple of streets away," he said. "I'm betting it was the bokor."

"Good work," Mark said. "At least one of you has his scent now. There's not much more we can do tonight. We'll head out first thing in the morning and canvas the other cemeteries. If we're lucky, we might be able to figure out where he plans to strike next."

As we drove through the city, I had the sudden sense of being watched. A new presence brushed my mind, paused in astonishment then latched onto me. The connection between us was far weaker than my bond to Reece or even my feeble link to the zombies. Whoever or whatever it was became aware that I knew they were in my mind. They pulled back before I could glean anything useful from them, other than a sense of excitement and horrid anticipation.

Highly disturbed by everything that had happened so far tonight, I decided to keep this to myself. I was already considered strange with my ability to sense zombies. There was no need to worry anyone unnecessarily with the possibility that another weird creature might be lurking in the city and that it seemed to be drawn to me.

Chapter Nine

Back in my room at last, I took a long shower to wash away the zombie ashes that coated me. It took three rinses to rid my hair of the smell of smoke. It was after midnight, but now that the ordeal was over, my hunger came back with a vengeance. The kitchen was calling to me, reminding me that I'd skipped dinner.

Forgoing coffee for once, I poured a glass of milk instead and made a peanut butter sandwich. It would have been weird sitting at the large dining table by myself, so I sat on one of the wooden bar stools that ran the length of the island counter instead. Without the TV on and with the rest of the squad asleep, the silence was stark.

Finishing my sandwich, I chugged down the milk and placed my dishes in the dishwasher. I felt Reece watching me before I turned to see him staring down at me through the coms room window on the second floor. I was dressed for bed in a thin white singlet and a tiny pair of pink sleeping shorts that barely covered my butt. His expression was inscrutable, but a flare of hunger escaped him before he clamped down on his emotions. I sensed that it wasn't food that he was craving.

I had the choice of either staying and listening to whatever he had to say, or fleeing outside through the door behind me. Running wasn't really an option, he'd easily catch me and I'd end up embarrassing myself. It would be better to just stay put and face the music.

Treading lightly, he descended the stairs and crossed the floor. Neither of us was bothered by the bare cement. My body temperature had risen since I'd become a shifter and the coolness felt nice against my bare feet.

"We need to talk," he said when he came to a stop a short distance away.

"About what?" I asked, playing dumb. The last thing I wanted to do was talk about our bond. I stood with my hands at my sides, feeling awkward in my sleepwear. Sure, he'd seen me naked, but this still felt too intimate. I had to struggle against the urge to cross my arms over my chest.

"About us. About our bond."

"There is no us," I replied. "The bond doesn't mean anything. It's just something that was forced on us due to unforeseen circumstances."

"You know it's more than that," he said in a low voice and took a step towards me.

I took two steps back and my heart was suddenly beating rapidly. "I know I'm the last person you wanted to sleep with," I said harshly. "You only touched me in the first place because Lust ordered you to."

His expression was impossible to read as he stared down at me. "Did I actually say that to you? That Lust specifically ordered me to have sex with someone that I wasn't attracted to?" he asked.

"No," I admitted. "I assumed that was what she ordered you to do. She only had two tricks, remember? She either forced people to find someone they despise and to sleep with them, or to find someone who despises them and to do the deed."

He frowned and looked away. I had the distinct feeling that I'd hurt him. "Of course. What other possible reason could there be for us to be together?" he said quietly, then turned and loped back up to the second floor.

I waited for his bedroom door to close before I took the stairs. Thankfully, our rooms were heavily soundproofed and no one heard me sob myself to sleep.

My eyes were red and puffy when my alarm woke me the next morning. I took a quick shower and applied makeup to hide the fact that I'd had a restless night. When I'd finally fallen asleep, I'd had nightmares about something stalking me. I vaguely remember running and running but the unknown creature just kept getting closer until I felt its putrid breath on my neck.

"Are you okay?" Kala asked as we were eating breakfast.

"I'm fine," I replied unconvincingly. "I just didn't sleep very well."

Reece glanced at me, but he kept his expression neutral. No doubt he thought he was the cause of my unrest. He was part of it, of course, but the nightmares had done their share as well.

Mark had gotten up early to map out our day. Leaving the flamethrowers in the back of the SUV, we carried our usual arsenal of handguns. The others hid their guns in the pockets of their cargo pants. I'd donned my red leather jacket this time, even though I'd be uncomfortably warm in it. It covered my holster well enough. My collection of clothing was scant and I'd have to ask Mark if he could have the rest of my wardrobe shipped to our base in Denver, since I had the feeling we'd spend more time there than anywhere else. I'd also see if he could retrieve my gun safe and the rest of my weapons.

We climbed into the SUV and Mark punched in the address of the first cemetery on our list. Driving at a far more sedate pace to avoid being pulled over by the police, Reece kept his eyes firmly on the road. He refrained from glancing at me in the rearview mirror.

A small voice in the back of my head told me I'd hurt his feelings last night, and I didn't know why. I'd only said the truth after all. Neither of us had asked to be bonded and we both wanted to escape from it. At least, I wanted to be free from the mental chains that were shackling me to him. I hated the idea of being tied to someone who hadn't chosen to be with me. Surely he felt the same way? Was his pride hurt that I'd only slept with him because I'd been compelled to? Why would that bother him when he'd admitted that he didn't even want me? Men were a strange species that I wasn't sure I'd ever understand.

We had fourteen more cemeteries to search and it was going to take all day. Being as inconspicuous as possible, we pulled up near the first graveyard and spread out to look for signs that the bokor was trying to raise an undead army. I was still too new to the job to be trusted to be on my own. Kala was my partner this time and she carried a camera as a prop as we pretended to be tourists. I carried a tattered map that I'd found in a drawer in the kitchen. It was Flynn's job to circle the perimeter of the grounds and see if he could pick up the Zombie King's scent again. It was my job to see if I could sense any zombies.

This cemetery was larger than the previous one, but I was already fairly certain that it was empty of the undead. No cold, scaly fingers dragged their way down my neck as we traversed from one side of the cemetery to the other.

We were all wearing earbuds to keep in contact with each other and I reported in to Mark when we were done. "The cemetery is clear," I said.

Flynn chimed in straight after me. "I'm not picking up anything. He hasn't been here recently." Apparently, we could pick up a scent that was several days old. We weren't as good as bloodhounds, but we were still pretty effective as trackers.

"Head back to the SUV," Mark instructed. Dressed in one of his usual dark suits, he had no chance of being able to blend in as a tourist. The rest of us were dressed in casual clothing. Kala was twenty-one and the two men were both twenty. They could all pass for college students, but I unfortunately still looked like I belonged in high school. It was lucky it was still the summer holidays and I hadn't been stopped by a cop to explain why I was truant.

We'd collected the cameras from where they'd been hidden before someone could find them and either steal them or call the police. If we'd had enough cameras to monitor each cemetery, we'd have simply installed them and then waited for the bokor to turn up on our computer screens. We were going to have to do this the hard way, by searching each graveyard in person.

Just as I'd thought, it took all day to traipse through each cemetery and to search for any signs of zombie activity. I shook my head at Mark when we drove to the final boneyard on his list. "I can't sense anything," I said as we pulled over.

Unhappy at our lack of success, he felt the need to search the grounds anyway. "It won't hurt to take a look around," he decided.

We met back at the SUV after Kala and I walked through the burial ground. Flynn had searched the perimeter for a familiar scent. "I didn't pick up any trace that he was here," he said.

"What now?" Reece asked our boss.

"Now we return to the base so I can hack into the CCTV cameras that surround the cemeteries," Mark replied. "Once I've done that, I can upload the link to my tablet." He always carried his tablet in a modified pocket inside his jacket. It was a very handy device.

"That's a clever idea," Kala said with genuine admiration for his tech skills.

"I thought so," he replied with something close to a smirk.

We'd stopped for lunch a few hours ago, but I was already hungry again. It was a little early for dinner when we returned to the compound, but I wasn't going to let that stop me. I cooked one of my favorite dishes, spaghetti bolognaise, and made sure there was enough for everyone.

"This is good," Flynn said in approval. It wasn't the first time I'd made the dish, but he always seemed surprised that my cooking was edible.

"It's much better than Kala's attempt at a cake," Reece joked.

I bit my bottom lip to contain my laugh at her splutter of outrage and made the mistake of glancing across the table at him. He wore a rare grin that made him seem young and carefree.

Kala elbowed me in the side and I realized I'd been staring. "I'd like to see you try to bake a cake," she grumbled. "I bet it turns out worse than mine."

"You're on," he said, accepting her challenge.

Flynn immediately grinned. "Mark's birthday is coming up soon, so you'll get your chance to dazzle us with your culinary skills."

All eyes shifted to Mark, who'd gone very still. "Sounds like a plan," he said with a weak smile. His expression hinted that he thought Reece would have as little success at cake making as Kala had.

"I'm sure Lexi will be happy to help you out," the blond said sweetly, then scowled when I stomped on her foot.

"I wouldn't want to put her out," Reece said curtly, concentrating on his meal rather than on me.

Chapter Ten

After dinner, Mark retreated to the coms room to hack into the cameras that surrounded the cemeteries. I tagged along to watch while he stood at the computer table. He only used two fingers to type, but he still managed to enter the commands quickly.

Monitors lined the walls on two sides of the table. They came to life and images appeared one by one as he took control of the CCTV camera feeds. Each of the graveyards came into view. Most of the entrances were covered, but there was always a chance that the Zombie King could sneak in through a side gate where we couldn't see him.

Mark entered a final command into the computer then stood back to watch his handiwork. "I've just set up a command that will alert us if movement is detected on any of the cameras," he explained.

"I guess we just have to wait for him to show up now," I said.

Keeping his attention on the screens, he nodded. "It can be quite tedious waiting for the bad guys to strike." He flicked a glance at me to see that I was far from excited by the prospect of watching the screens for what might turn out to be several hours before anything happened. "I had a laptop delivered to the compound while we were busy searching the cemeteries. You can use it to search through the PIA archives, if you like." That news immediately perked me up. "Some files are restricted and you won't be able to open them, but you'll find plenty of interesting information that might come in handy."

He nodded towards the coffee table behind me and I turned to see a shiny silver laptop sitting there in plain sight. I was chagrined that I hadn't even noticed it. So much for my observation skills.

Striding over, I picked it up and grinned. "Thanks, boss," I said. It felt strange calling him that, but I was sure I'd get used to it soon enough.

"Make sure you don't spend all night trawling through the files," he called after me as I headed for my room. "I want you to get a decent night's sleep."

"Whatever you say, Mom," I called back and was pretty sure he chuckled.

Pushing open my bedroom door, I closed then locked it before heading for my bed. I piled pillows behind my back, then switched the computer on. I spent a few minutes familiarizing myself with the programs then clicked on a folder that had been named 'Archives'. Thousands of files appeared. It would take me months, if not years, to read through them all and I didn't know where to start. I decided that starting at the beginning would make the most sense. It helped that the files were listed both chronologically and also by topic.

The first file contained scanned copies of handwritten pages that had been taken from an ancient notebook. The book must have been several hundred years old, judging by the archaic style of writing. A handy modern translation had been added beneath each page.

Reading through the documents, I became lost in a tale of demon possession in England from over four hundred years ago. A priest had been called on to try to save a teenage girl after her personality had undergone a wild transformation. She'd gone from being a demure, well behaved young lady to a depraved, evil horror.

The priest's description of the spirit that had taken over the girl's young body was chilling. He'd been quite the artist and several drawings were included in the file. One was of a pretty girl that looked just a few years younger than me. She was sleeping peacefully with her hand curled beside her face and her long, dark hair spread out around her.

In the next picture, her eyes were wild and her face was a rictus of evil. The third drawing was enough to give me nightmares. The child was gone and a hideous demon had taken her place. Larger than a man, he towered over a group of cowering people. Large, leathery wings sprouted from his back and horns rose from his forehead. His tongue was forked and his pupils were vertically slit, like a goat. He was naked, fully aroused and had an appendage large enough to cause a woman permanent damage. Cloven feet finished off his hideous visage.

I read through the account of how the priest had banished the demon through a combination of prayer, holy water and religious artifacts. His faith in God had been his strongest weapon and he'd finally driven the spirit back to the fiery realm where he belonged.

The priest had been the first member of an organization that had eventually blossomed into the current Paranormal Investigation Agency. He'd recruited other men and women who'd come into contact with supernatural beings and had lived to tell the tale. They'd carried on his work after he'd died. Once America had become more populated, the organization had quickly spread here as well. Monsters existed everywhere and the PIA had branches all over the world.

It was past my usual bedtime by the time I finished reading the account of demon possession. Sleep was going to be hard to come by after reading that account of horror. The demon had been summoned by the girl's mother for reasons unknown to the priest. She'd used her daughter as both a sacrifice and a conduit for the demon to become corporeal. The poor kid had been torn apart during the process.

The mother had underestimated the power of the creature that she'd summoned and she'd quickly lost control of him. His first act of free will had been to kill her. The demon hadn't stopped at just destroying her. He'd ended up raping and killing several other people in her small village before the priest had finally cornered and then banished him.

Readying myself for bed, I couldn't get the image of the demon out of my mind. Switching off the light didn't plunge the room into darkness for me anymore. My night sight was now good enough to light up the room in a soft glow. I wasn't sure I'd want to be in a completely dark room with the images that were implanted in my head.

I climbed between the sheets, closed my eyes and they immediately sprang open again when I saw the snarling face of the demon behind my eyelids. Maybe it wasn't such a good idea to read through the old files just before I went to bed.

Gradually, the image faded and so did my fright. Just before I slipped off to sleep I realized that Reece was sending me calming thoughts. My agitation had been keeping him awake as well.

I slept through the night, which meant the bokor hadn't attempted to raise a fresh batch of zombies. If he had, we'd have been roused out of our beds and driven back to New Orleans.

Mark beckoned me over to the table when I headed downstairs for breakfast. He was kind enough to wait for me to grab a bowl of cereal before speaking.

"Now that you're a permanent member of the team, I want to make sure you receive enough training to keep you safe from the things that we hunt."

I'd been expecting this talk and I was tentatively excited by the prospect of learning more skills. "What sort of training do you have in mind?"

"Obviously, you won't require any tutelage when it comes to guns." We shared a smile at that. "I'd like you to learn how to use a variety of other weapons and hand to hand combat techniques. You might be strong and fast, but there are creatures out there that are even more dangerous than shifters." His expression turned grave as he presumably remembered something that he and his team had encountered before I'd come along. "Kala, Flynn and Reece all have their own unique skills. I'd like you to spend at least eight hours every day training with them until you're up to speed."

Nodding in agreement, I squelched my unhappiness at being teamed up with Reece. He'd probably feel just as uncomfortable to be in close proximity with me during our training sessions.

He saw through my false calm to the root of my problem. "You're much stronger than a normal teenager now," he said. "Reece will be the best person to assist you to learn control so you don't accidentally hurt any humans."

Kala had ambled into the kitchen during our conversation and she joined us carrying a mug of coffee. "It's about time we had another female on the team. It'll be fun to teach you how to fight with knives, stakes and other types of weapons as well as hand to hand combat."

Her enthusiasm was infectious and I grinned. I'd always been interested in martial arts, but I'd never stayed in one place long enough to bother taking any classes.

"Yeah," Flynn agreed dourly. "It's fun right up until you get a knife in the face." He sent a wry look at Kala as he took the seat across from her with a brimming bowl of cereal.

"Sheesh," she complained. "That happened two years ago! You have to let it go and move on."

"You almost took my eye out!"

She waved her hand carelessly. "I motivated you to move faster, didn't I?"

"Are they always like this?" I asked Mark as the pair continued to squabble.

"Yes," Reece said as he descended to the bottom of the stairs. "They're worse than children." He had dark circles beneath his eyes and I knew I was the cause of his unrest.

"I'm older than you, Rex," Kala reminded him and his nose wrinkled at the hated nickname.

"Only physically," he countered smoothly. "Mentally, I'd say you're about fifteen."

"*I'm* fifteen?" she said and bounded to her feet in outrage. "At least I'm not pining away for…"

She trailed off when I pushed my chair back and stood. I wasn't sure why I'd been drawn into their argument, but she'd just crossed the line pointing out my hopeless crush. "I'm going to my room to read for a while," I said to Mark dully. He sent me a sympathetic glance then glared at Kala.

"Lexi, I didn't mean…" she reached for me, but I dodged away from her and walked over to the stairs. Climbing the stairs fast enough to make myself dizzy, I strode down the hall and into my room. I locked the door to keep out any unwanted intruders, then leaned back against it and forced my tears away. She was right, which was why her jibe had hurt so much. I was acting like a lovesick little girl and it was time for me to grow up.

The bond told me that Reece was furious with Kala. His rage beat in my temples, bringing me to the verge of a headache. Little by little, I pushed his emotions away until I was alone in my head again. Feeling calmer now, I settled onto the bed and opened the laptop to begin reading the next file in the PIA archives.

Flynn was the only one downstairs when I stopped to take a break for lunch. He was making coffee and lifted an empty mug in silent enquiry.

"I'd love one," I said in answer to his unspoken question.

"How are you feeling?" he asked when he filled my mug and pushed it across the counter to me.

I shrugged and spooned one sugar into the mixture. "I'm okay. A little embarrassed, but otherwise fine."

"You do know that Kala wasn't talking about you, right?"

He searched my face, which no doubt reflected my surprise at his statement. "Of course she was talking about me."

"Actually, she wasn't," he corrected me. "She was talking about Garrett."

I shook my head in denial, almost spilling cream all over the counter. This time, I managed to direct the flow into my mug, but only because of my freaky new reflexes. "Whatever he feels for me isn't real. It's just a byproduct of Lust's compulsion and the bond that was forced on us both."

"Hmm," he mused and took a sip of coffee. "Then how do you explain his attraction for you before Lust took over his mind?"

I was too startled to respond and he walked away before I could come up with an answer.

After another hour or so reading, my embarrassment had faded and I decided it was time to face the others. I couldn't learn how to fight by staying in my room. Kala was sitting on the couch flicking through a magazine when I descended the stairs again. Reece and Flynn were sparring in the boxing ring. They were hitting each other hard enough to leave marks that would fade within minutes. If they hit a normal human that hard, they'd have broken their bones or ruptured their internal organs.

Kala sent me a cautious glance when I came to a stop in front of her. "About what I said earlier," she began.

I waved her apology away before she could finish. "Don't worry about it. I'd rather not talk about the subject at all, if that's okay with you."

Her smile was relieved and she acceded to my request. "What type of training do you want to tackle first?" she asked. She knew me well enough to know that I wasn't mad at her anymore.

"I feel like stabbing something," I replied and she grinned.

"Maybe we should find somewhere else to train," Flynn whispered to his sparring partner loudly enough for us to hear him.

Kala flipped him the bird and stood. "Come on, we'll train outside so the boys don't get too turned on by seeing us hot chicks in action."

I felt Reece's amusement like a caress in my mind and strengthened the barrier that I'd constructed between us. It was hard to keep him out, but it wasn't impossible. In time, maybe we'd learn to mask each other's thoughts and feelings well enough that we could forget that the bond even existed.

Chapter Eleven

It took three more nights before the bokor was caught on camera entering one of the cemeteries. It was late and I was deeply asleep when a noise woke me. Realizing someone was pounding on the door, I stumbled out of bed and opened it.

Mark stood on the other side. He didn't look as if he'd been to bed at all. "The bokor has just appeared in one of the cemeteries," he said. "Get dressed and meet us in the garage. We're leaving in five minutes."

Suddenly wide awake, I quickly pulled on the clothes I'd laid out just in case I had to move fast. My sniper rifle wouldn't be needed this time, so I left it behind. The pockets of my cargo pants were already loaded with my handgun and spare ammo. Our SUV was loaded up with flamethrowers and fuel. I took a few moments to run a brush through my hair and to pull it up into a ponytail before leaving my room and sprinting for the garage.

Mark was the last to arrive. As always, he wore a dark suit. He'd teamed it up with a crisp white business shirt and a tie. He was a federal agent from his short, thinning brown hair to his shiny black shoes. The rest of us were wearing casual clothes of cargo pants and t-shirts.

We zoomed to the highway and we reached New Orleans in record time. Speeding through the dark, mostly empty streets, we pulled up short of the cemetery where the Zombie King had been spotted. Mark zapped the cameras so we wouldn't be caught on tape and we hurried closer.

Well before we entered the gate, I knew we'd arrived too late. "I think they're gone," I said to Mark.

He stopped and gathered us into a circle. "You can't sense them in the cemetery anymore?"

I shook my head and peered into the gloom. Green fog permeated the area again, but it was already dissipating. "I can sense that they were here, but I think they left a few minutes ago." If the compound had been just a few miles closer, we'd have arrived in time to catch the Zombie King before he'd escaped.

"This whole place reeks of zombie," Kala pointed out. "They should be easy enough to follow."

Mark motioned for Reece to take point and the rest of us fell in behind him. Clutching my flamethrower tightly, I searched the shadows for the undead. I was ready to fire at anything that jumped out and tried to eat me.

We moved through the rows and came to the epicenter of where the minions had been raised. Reece pointed at a bloody circle on the ground. "The bokor didn't bother to hide his ritual circle this time," he said.

Mark used his cell phone to take a photo of the grisly symbols. They'd been drawn in blood, human blood most likely. Like his predecessors, he documented each case that his team was involved in and he'd later add it to the archives. He took photos of the gaping crypts as well.

"They went this way," Reece said and pointed towards the gate at the rear of the grounds.

I knew the zombies and their master were long gone, but we did our best to follow them anyway. The bokor had called another thirty minions forth before vacating the cemetery. Maybe thirty was his limit.

We lost their trail in a side street one block away from the cemetery.

"He must have loaded them into a truck," Flynn said.

"I wonder what he's planning to use them for?" Kala said. Her tone was frustrated.

Mark was just as mystified. "There's no way to know until after he makes his move," he replied softly. "We need to find him and stop him before he causes havoc."

Thirty zombies didn't sound like much of an army to me, but it was our job to catch the bad guys and it was doubtful that the bokor had raised the corpses with the intention of performing charity work.

We patrolled the city with the hope that I'd be able to sense the zombies, but had no luck. By morning, the cops would be aware that something strange was going on. They'd find the empty crypts and the bloody symbols on the ground. Some of them would suspect the truth, but most would just assume that it was kids playing a prank. They'd put more men and women on patrol, which would make our job all the more difficult. We tended to work on the fringes rather than out in the open. The PIA wouldn't be very clandestine if the general population knew that we existed.

Reece angled the SUV back towards the compound. He drove along the mostly deserted highway so quickly that we were just a blur to the few other motorists. I was more than ready for bed by the time I slipped between the sheets again. Not even a skilled bokor could compel his undead henchmen to attack anyone during daylight hours. The city would be safe until sunset the next night.

Mark had a surprise for me when I dragged myself out of bed late the next morning. Still half asleep, I was eating breakfast when he dropped something on the table in front of me. Picking up the small black wallet, I flipped it open to see myself staring back. The upper half of the wallet had a yellow circle with

Federal Agent in bold yellow letters in the middle. Much smaller beneath it was the initials PIA. I had no idea when he'd taken the photo of me, but my face was somber and unsmiling, just like his ID. It stated that I was Agent Alexis Levine.

I grinned and slipped the ID into my pocket. "Now I feel like I'm really part of the team," I said.

"You've been a part of the team since the day I picked you up in Texas," he said as he made himself a fresh cup of coffee. "The ID just formalizes your status."

Our initial arrangement was only supposed to be temporary, but now I couldn't go back to my old life. I mused over my status as an agent as I finished breakfast. I wasn't old enough to drink yet, but I was a member of an elite team that hunted down monsters. I glossed over the fact that I was a monster myself. That was a detail I wasn't yet comfortable with and might never be.

"All right, Agent Levine," Flynn said from the boxing ring. "Let's see what you've learned so far." His expression was mischievous as he bounced lightly on the balls of his feet. I was glad to see him wearing boxing gloves this time. Being punched in the face with a gloved fist hurt far less than being hit with bare knuckles.

Reece was working out with the weights and Kala stood beside the ring, ready to officiate. She threw me a pair of gloves that were far too large for my small hands. "Go get 'em, tiger," she said with a wink. That struck me as funny, since she was the only feline in our group.

My grin faded when I stepped into the ring and Flynn immediately went on the attack. For a few moments, I ducked, weaved and blocked his punches as best I could. When he landed a punch on my chin, I saw stars and almost went down. The pain only lasted for a few moments, but it ignited a white hot anger that I'd never felt before. Blocking his next blow, I punched him in the ribs as hard as I could and heard a bone snap.

He hunched over with a grunt of pain and Walker let out a whoop of laughter. "Way to go, Lexi!" she said with a grin.

A broken bone took longer to heal than bruises and I had to wait for the color to return to Flynn's face before we could resume our match.

"That was pretty good," he said. He was far more wary now that I'd unleashed my irritation on him. "Just try not to let your anger take over, or you'll lose your focus."

I knew what he meant and I tried to rein in the rage that was pounding inside my head. It was a mystery where it had come from. Then I made the mistake of glancing at Reece and the mystery was solved. He was glaring at my sparring partner as he pumped weights. I snuck a peek through the bond to feel him seething with ire. He didn't like seeing me get hurt and he was doing his best to control himself.

Clamping down on the bond again, I pushed aside the anger that didn't even belong to me and focused on learning as much as I could during my session.

Being a shifter, it took a lot of activity to exhaust me now. Even after hours of sparring, I was still bursting with energy. I took a shower while Mark cooked dinner. We were eating early so we could head back to the city to search for the bokor and his undead soldiers.

Mark's taste in food was varied and he served us a stir-fry that was as good as anything I'd eaten in a restaurant anywhere. Piling our dishes into the dishwasher, we retrieved our weapons and trooped out to the garage. The sun was still an hour from setting when we left the compound and Reece drove at a pace that was sedate for him.

"Circle the city before you enter it," Mark instructed. "Let's see if we can pick up any trace of the bokor and his zombies."

It was going to be difficult to pick up their trail if they were in a truck as we suspected. Once we were close enough to them, my strange zombie radar would hopefully be able to pinpoint their location.

Chapter Twelve

We cruised around the edges of New Orleans as the sun receded from the sky and darkness took over. I was on high alert for the telltale presence of zombies. Cars thronged the streets, slowing us down. We drove past all fifteen cemeteries, but I didn't sense any more walking dead being summoned from their resting places.

After a couple of hours of patrolling, we stopped for gas and took the opportunity to stretch our legs. A tickle at the back of my head made me turn to see who was watching. I sensed the unknown presence again. The link between us seemed to be strengthening, which was a frightening prospect since I didn't even know who or what it was. Its thoughts were still largely muffled, but I sensed that its interest in me was increasing.

Mark was standing next to Reece as he filled the tank. They were conversing quietly about our mission. Kala was pretending that a pair of guys weren't staring at her, but it was obvious that she was well aware of their eyes on her butt. Flynn was washing the windscreen that had become filthy from our trips to and from the compound.

No one else was aware that we were being observed. I was beginning to wonder if it was all just in my head when I was distracted by a large truck that ambled past. My head whipped around to follow the vehicle as it rounded the corner. It was carrying a cargo of reanimated corpses in the back.

"The bokor just drove past us with a truck full of zombies," I called to the others and received a strange look from a woman who was filling her tank ahead of us.

Reece hurriedly finished up while Mark paid for the gas. Another car drove up to box us in as we climbed into the SUV. We had to wait for the woman to return to her car and waited impatiently as she checked her reflection and touched up her lipstick. Reece put his hand on the horn and held it down until she glared at him in the rearview mirror and finally started her car. Upset at rudely being urged to move, she took her time to ease into the traffic.

"The truck turned right at the corner," I said. I was sitting on the edge of the seat, straining to pick up the trail as we followed in the truck's wake.

We sped down the street and were stopped at the next light. By the time it turned green, the last residue of zombie had faded from my senses. "I lost the trail," I said in disappointment.

"At least we know the bokor is in town and that he brought his minions with him," Mark replied. "Keep driving around until Lexi senses them again," he instructed.

By the time I sensed the undead again, we were too late to stop the Zombie King from unleashing his plan. I felt the disturbing buzzing in my head, but this time the corpses weren't longing for food. They'd already found it. "They're just ahead," I warned and pointed to a bank standing on the corner.

Driving past the building, we peered through the windows to see only darkness inside. We turned the corner and pulled to a stop in the mouth of an alley at the back of the bank. The back door had been pulled off its hinges and lay on the ground. Half a dozen zombies were on their hands and knees, hunkered over an unmoving body. I could only see part of the dead human, but it looked like he was wearing a uniform. He was most likely a security guard. A silent alarm had probably been tripped when the back door had been broken into. The guard had made the biggest mistake of his life when he'd come to investigate.

"We need to take care of them before the police arrive," Mark said. He made a quick call to the local Cleanup Crew and we climbed out of the SUV. The zombies sensed me and bared their bloody teeth. These walking dead were in about the same condition as the ones we'd roasted last night, but their meal seemed to be giving them strength. Hissing, they stood and began to shamble towards us.

"They really don't like you," Kala murmured as they fixed their milky eyes on me.

"The feeling is mutual," I replied as Flynn opened the back door of the SUV and reached for a flamethrower. Reece grabbed one as well and the pair stepped into the alley to send a wall of fire at the approaching monstrosities.

I shut down my tenuous link to the undead minions as they shrieked in agony. Flailing and burning, they fell down and became crispy corpses just as a dark gray van pulled up at the far end of the alley.

"Do you sense any more zombies in the area?" Mark asked.

I shook my head, relieved that the momentary pain in my mind was fading. "I think the bokor left these six behind to slow us down. The rest of them aren't anywhere nearby."

"I'm going to take a look inside," he said. "Keep watch and let me know if the police turn up." He skirted around the still smoldering skeletons then turned and crooked his finger at me. "Bring a flamethrower, just in case."

Flynn handed me his weapon and I took it with a nod of thanks. I had no idea why Agent Steel wanted me to accompany him inside the bank, but I wasn't about to question him. I was right on his heels as he stepped over the heavy metal door that bore smeared handprints. Forensic testing would determine that the black goo was rotting human flesh. I noticed a broken camera above where the door had been.

My stride wasn't as long as Mark's and I had to jump over the door. The floor was filthy with what my nose was telling me was chunks of zombie flesh. The smell of decomposing meat was unmistakable. While the Zombie King's dark magic could reanimate bodies, it apparently couldn't stop the inevitable rot.

Doors branched off to either side of the hallway that stretched out ahead of us. I spied another broken camera dangling from a couple of wires. Pieces of plastic and metal littered the floor.

We found the vault halfway down on the right. Again, the heavy metal door had been torn off its hinges and was smeared with noisome splotches. "How strong are zombies?" I asked, awed that they could so easily break metal doors down.

"Very," Mark replied as he entered the room. I was impressed again by the construction of the mausoleums in the local cemeteries. The strongest ones could apparently withstand being battered by their undead occupants and suffer little to no damage.

The vault itself was untouched, but dozens of deposit boxes had been ripped from the walls and then ransacked. It didn't look like the bokor had been after anything specific. He'd rifled through the boxes and had taken what he wanted, leaving less valuable items behind.

A small, square metal table sat in the middle of the room. Two uncomfortable plastic chairs had been provided for customers to sit on. A white card emblazoned with a red skull and crossbones had been placed precisely in the center of the table. Mark picked it up and examined the other side. 'Zombie King' had been typed in a font that was supposed to mimic blood.

"He left a calling card?" I said incredulously. If he wanted the cops to know who he was, why bother to break the cameras? Like so many other thieves, he was a coward at heart.

Mark nodded and pocketed the card. "It appears that the bokor is seeking infamy as well as fortune." Sirens sounded in the distance and his cell phone beeped in warning as one of his agents sent him a message. "That's our cue to leave," he said and hastened outside.

The Cleanup Crew had piled all six of the crispy corpses as well as the dead security guard into the back of their van. They'd scrubbed the alley as clean as they could and were wiping the zombie residue from the discarded metal door when we hurried past them. One of the Crew was female, but she was almost as tall as her male partner. Her shoulders might actually be a fraction wider than his. Both wore dark blue overalls. They nodded in greeting and I nodded back.

"Thank you for your assistance," Mark said to the pair.

"It's our job, Agent Steel," the male crew member said amiably enough. He was in his early forties and had a deep, gravelly voice and a nose that was skewed to one side.

"Someone has to clean up after your squad," the female said in amusement. Her hair was light brown and it was just long enough to put up into a ponytail. They were chattier than the Crew from Denver, but we didn't have time to talk. They were hurrying inside the bank to wipe away all traces of the undead robbers when we motored away.

We circled the block a couple of times and the dark gray van was gone on our second circuit. The cops arrived on our third trip around to the back alley. A midnight blue sedan was parked around the back of the bank and two plainclothes police officers were approaching the doorway with their guns drawn. One was older, short and balding. The other was younger, handsome and blond. I wondered what they'd make of the robbery and if they'd ever learn the real truth of who and what had broken into the bank. If they did, their lives would never be the same again.

Chapter Thirteen

After leaving the bank, we drove in random patterns around New Orleans, hoping to pick up the Zombie King's trail. Frustrated and cranky, we eventually gave up and headed back to our base. The bokor had to be hiding somewhere outside of town. There were far too many places to search effectively with just our small team. We'd have to wait for him to strike again and hope that we'd have better luck catching him in the act next time.

Determined to sleep in, I was woken far too early when a fist banged on the door. Kala's grin widened when she saw my bloodshot eyes and annoyance at being woken so early. "Rise and shine," she sang. "It's time to train!"

"I need breakfast first," I grumbled and shut the door on her smirk. I took a quick shower and dressed in my usual white tank top and a ratty pair of sweatpants. Now that everyone knew about the scars on both of my shoulders, there was no point in trying to hide them.

I discovered Reece was of the same opinion when I stomped down the spiral staircase to the kitchen. He was working out in the gym and wore only a pair of cutoff jeans. Even from all the way across the gigantic room, I could see the scar that I'd left on him. His eyes flicked up to meet mine a second before I turned away. Irreversibly marked both physically and mentally, neither of us could escape from the trap of our bond.

Joining Kala and Mark at the table, I took my time eating my cereal. While I felt full of energy when I was on a mission, I needed more than four or five hours of sleep to recharge. None of the others were feeling the effects of driving around for half the night. Coffee helped to restore me a little more before I forced myself to join Kala in the boxing ring.

Two inches taller than my opponent, I was less heavily muscled and far less skilled than her. Her solid frame should have made her slower than me, but her reflexes were uncannily quick and precise. Her stare was focused and downright frightening in its intensity. Now I knew what a mouse felt like when it was being stalked by a cat.

Receiving a punch to my solar plexus, I went down to one knee, struggling to breathe. Kala laughed in glee and danced back a couple of steps. The white hot rage flared within me and I went after her. Her amusement changed to alarm when she saw that I wasn't kidding around. I swung a punch at her head and she ducked just in time. She had to dodge and weave to keep out of my reach as I went on the offensive rather than the defensive for a change.

"Channel the anger, or you'll do something you'll regret," Reece said, distracting me momentarily. He and Flynn were standing beside the ring, watching us spar.

"She's too slow to actually land a punch," Kala scoffed and grinned at me cheekily. My rage flared again and I noted that my emotions were heightened by Reece's anger. Most of the time he kept it banked, but every now and then it flowed over. Silently, he showed me how to use my rage to heighten my reflexes. Letting him guide me, I faked a punch to Kala's ribs with my left fist. As she dropped her hands to deflect the blow, I lashed out with my right hand and my glove connected with her jaw.

Dazed by the punch, she stumbled back a step. Her sign of weakness ignited my instinct to attack and I unleashed a bevy of punches at her. Gone was my ability to control myself and I swung wild blows that weren't very well aimed. I landed a lucky punch and she went down to her knees. Hands caught me around my middle and I was yanked off my feet and pulled up against a rock hard chest.

Thoughts of fighting were instantly replaced with thoughts of a carnal nature when Reece spoke into my ear. "You need to learn control," he said as Flynn knelt beside Kala. "You're not a child anymore."

His cold pronouncement was like a bucket of icy water to the face and my anger drained away. Blood was trickling from Kala's split lip and guilt hit me. I struggled free and crouched beside her. Flynn's glare was just short of hostile.

"I'm sorry," I said contritely. "Are you okay?"

Shaking her head to clear it, she offered me a feeble grin and wiped the blood away with her sleeve. She left a smear of red on the white t-shirt. "I'm fine. That'll teach me to underestimate you."

"What the hell is wrong with you?" Flynn asked me in disapproval.

"Don't look at me," I defended myself. "Most of that anger wasn't even mine." We all turned to look at Reece.

He shrugged and I had to look away as another surge of what I could only describe as lust swept through me at his half naked state. "It's not my fault that you can sometimes feel my emotions," he reasoned.

"It kind of is," Kala argued. "You bonded with her and now you'll have to learn to control your inner rage so it doesn't spill over onto Lexi."

It didn't surprise me that the pair knew of his private turmoil. They'd known him for almost their entire lives. They knew things about him that I'd probably never learn myself. I might be a member of the squad, but I'd always be a latecomer to their tightknit family.

"Didn't Mark say you'd be the best person to teach Lexi control?" Flynn said.

"Yeah," Reece replied with a heavy sigh.

"Then maybe you could spare some time to do so, so we don't get our heads torn off by a rampaging werewolf."

"I wasn't on a rampage," I said sulkily.

"You were on the verge of it," Kala said and held her hand out to me.

Standing, I drew her to her feet. Her lip had stopped bleeding and she was thankfully showing no signs of a concussion. We healed too fast to be down for long.

"You could have wiped the floor with me if you really wanted to," I said with a frown. Why were they making such a big deal out of this? I'd briefly lost my temper and had bopped her in the mouth. It wasn't like I tore one of her arms off.

"You don't know much about shifters yet," Reece said, picking up on that thought. He took the gloves that Kala handed him. "You have no idea what we're really capable of."

Flynn lifted the rope high enough for Kala to step out of the ring, then climbed out after her. "Each shifter has different attributes," he explained. "For instance, my reptilian nature means I have more patience than most of our kind."

It was Kala's turn to speak up next. "I tend to play with my prey and draw out the kill, unless Mark is there to keep me focused." That wasn't much of a shock. I'd seen cats stalking their food and they could be unbelievably cruel.

"What about werewolves?" I asked. "What are we like?"

Balancing on the balls of his bare feet, Reece fielded that one. "We tend to lose control faster and more often than other shifters. If we allow ourselves to become angry, we can be downright vicious. It's almost impossible to stop us from tearing our enemies apart once we reach a certain point."

The blood drained out of my face, leaving me white and trembling. Not only did my wolf nature make me susceptible to anger, I also had his emotions inside my head. How was I supposed to remain in control when the odds were so heavily stacked against me?

Reading that thought, he had an answer. "I'm going to help you learn to balance your emotions."

For the next couple of hours, he goaded me into anger, then helped me to swallow it back down and regain focus again. I was drenched with sweat and was exhausted from concentrating on keeping my emotions in check when he finally called a halt to our session. "That's enough for today. Let's take a break for lunch."

My stomach rumbled at the reminder and Reece cracked a rare smile. His skin glistened with sweat and I clamped down on the urge to lean forward and lick his chest. I turned away as my face flamed, positive that he'd caught either the image or the thought.

Standing next to the coffee machine in the kitchen, Kala saw my red face and her shoulders moved in silent mirth. She didn't need to read my mind to know what I was thinking. Thankfully, she kept her snide remarks to herself for once.

Chapter Fourteen

After lunch, I received weapons training from Kala and Flynn. I spent a couple of hours slashing at a plastic dummy that they'd dragged out of storage and had propped up in the corner. It was the same kind of dummy that was used in crash testing. It was durable enough to survive being stabbed repeatedly by someone with even my strength.

While I wasn't particularly skilled with knives, I was starting to pick up the basics. Becoming a supernatural creature hadn't given me magical fighting prowess. It would take months before I'd become competent and years before I'd be able to hold my own against the others.

"Now it's your turn to teach us," Kala said after I finished cutting up the plastic man to her satisfaction.

"I'll see if Mark wants to join the session." She darted away before I could protest at being thrust into the role of a teacher.

Reece had disappeared upstairs sometime during my knife training so I was left with just Flynn for company. He'd offered me some pointers during the session, but I sensed he was still annoyed with me for losing control of my temper. "I'm really sorry for going after Kala like that," I said in a small voice.

Letting out a quiet sigh, he put his arm around my shoulders and drew me in for a quick hug. "I know. I'm not really mad at you, Lexi. I just wish you hadn't been caught up in this life in the first place. If Garrett had been able to control himself…" He trailed off without finishing his sentence.

"You don't know how horrible it was to fall under Lust's spell," I said, haunted by my utter lack of memory at the contact I'd had with her. "She takes away your ability to think and you have no choice but to do whatever she says." Not that I could recall what she'd said to me. I just had Reece's word to go on and he hadn't been very forthcoming with the details.

"I get that," he said and lowered his voice as he checked that the others were still upstairs. "But she didn't command him to bite you, did she?"

"Well, no," I replied. "She didn't know he was a shifter."

"So why did he bite you?" Flynn's stare drilled into me, seeking answers.

123

"It was the night of the full moon and his instincts kicked in." It was a feeble answer, but it was the only one I had.

"You might be more right than you realize," he said and dropped his voice even more until it was a bare whisper. "I think he bit you because his wolf didn't want to be alone anymore."

All the breath left my body, leaving me feeling light headed. "Are you saying that he marked me on purpose?"

His nod was slow and thoughtful. "That's my theory."

"But why choose me?" Denver had been full of attractive girls. Surely he'd have chosen one of them over me. "He doesn't even like me."

"Are you sure about that?" he asked with one eyebrow raised in disbelief. "Maybe he just told you that to keep you at a distance."

Footsteps clattered on the spiral staircase, interrupting our conversation. Could he be right? Had Reece bonded with me deliberately? It seemed highly unlikely given what I sensed from him through our link. I didn't feel anything but guilt, unhappiness and the occasional flare of lust. Besides, he'd made a point of telling me he didn't want me and that I wasn't his type.

Mark was right behind Kala, but descended the stairs at a more sedate pace. I was surprised when Reece trailed after them. He'd donned shoes and a tight black t-shirt that fitted him like a second skin.

Calming my mind like he'd taught me, I pushed away my attraction to him as Mark beckoned for us to follow him. If it could work to subdue anger, I hoped it could also control desire.

"Kala informs me you're about to hold a training session," he said as he opened the door to the long hallway that led to the garage and the other rooms.

"That's the plan," I said, hiding my nervousness at the prospect of training my trainers. I'd never had students before, apart from giving out a few pointers here and there.

Flynn smiled, putting aside his earlier anger. "This should be fun. I've always wanted to be taught how to shoot by a teenager."

I rolled my eyes, but refrained from making a snide comment. While I wasn't comfortable with the role of an instructor, I'd attempt to be as professional as possible. We filed into the indoor gun range and the team selected handguns from the collection hanging on pegs on the wall. Hundreds of boxes of ammunition were stored in the cupboards beneath the weapons and they loaded up their guns of choice.

"How do you want to do this?" Mark asked.

"Why don't each of you take turns shooting off a few rounds so I can see your skill levels?" I already had a firm idea of their abilities, but we had to start somewhere.

"I'll go first," Kala offered. I'd spent a few sessions at both the indoor and outdoor ranges with her and her skill had already improved with my assistance. She had no problems accepting my help. She blasted off a few rounds, hitting the paper target of a man through the heart with four of her five shots. "Am I awesome or what?" she crowed. Modesty would never be her forte.

"That's pretty good," I conceded. Previously, she'd have been lucky to hit the heart with two of the five shots at the one hundred yard mark. The more distant the target was, the harder it was to hit accurately.

Flynn went next. He took his time and grouped his shots nicely. I nodded in approval, taking note that we'd have to work on his speed rather than his precision. Mark gripped his gun tightly and flicked the barrel up slightly after each shot, causing his aim to deviate a little. He was an okay shot at close range, but from further than fifty feet away, he had trouble. Reece went last and aimed almost lazily. He hit the heart all five times, then cocked his eyebrows in silent query. I couldn't fault his aim and nodded in mute praise.

During the next hour, I spent time with each of my team mates, helping them to improve their skills. Kala just needed more practice and to learn to have a little more patience. Flynn managed to speed up with my urging, but his aim became less precise. With he, he'd learn to balance the two.

Mark eventually stopped jerking his arms, but it was going to take a lot of practice to drum that into him. Reece didn't really need my help. I touched his shoulder to correct his stance once and heat instantly flared between us. Flynn bit his bottom lip to hide his grin and Kala glanced over at us with a smirk. Our boss was oblivious to the byplay since he didn't have a shifter's instincts.

I should have been exhausted after eight hours of training, but I was feeling energized as the sun began to sink and we settled in for an early dinner. I'd recovered from my one on one session with Reece fairly quickly after it had no longer been necessary to concentrate as fiercely.

It was Kala's turn to cook, which meant we were eating frozen pizza again. I decided to offer her cooking lessons once our mission was over and we had time to relax.

"I spent the day searching CCTV footage for the truck that the bokor stole," Mark said between bites of his subpar pizza.

"Did you have any luck?" Reece asked.

Mark waggled his hand from side to side. "A little. The vehicle entered from the west, but left via the north."

"The Zombie King is smarter than we thought," Kala said with her mouth full. It was fascinating and horrifying to watch her eat and talk at the same time. My father had taught me better manners than that. Mark gave her a long-suffering look, but didn't bother to berate her.

Kala was on my left and Mark was at the head of the table. Reece sat across from me with Flynn to his right. It was our usual seating arrangement and it was strangely homey to be sharing a meal and discussing work at the same time. I'd never imagined that I'd become a federal agent for an organization that no one had ever heard of, yet here I was. I had to admit that I enjoyed the work far more than I'd have thought possible. So far anyway.

"I'd prefer it if he was stupid," Flynn grumbled. "It'd make it a lot easier to catch him."

Reece nodded in agreement. "He could be hiding out anywhere outside the city. We'll never be able to track him down."

"We'll just have to stick to the plan and try to catch him in the act," our boss said.

Kala shook her head and swallowed before speaking this time. "I still can't believe this guy raised a bunch of zombies to rob a bank."

"I guess it's better than using them to take control of New Orleans and force everyone to become his slaves," I offered.

"That'll come when he gains enough experience to raise an entire cemetery," Mark said.

I waited for someone to laugh at the joke, but no one did. "Are you serious?" My tone went higher than usual and was almost a squeak.

"Practitioners of the black arts crave attention, recognition and power," Reece said. "Now that the bokor has had a taste of what he can do, it won't be long before he'll move on to bigger and better sport. Why rob banks when you can hold an entire city hostage?"

His reasoning was sound and I pictured the unknown bokor sitting on a throne made of stacks of money. In my imagination, scantily clad, terrified women cowered at his feet. Reece's lips moved upwards fractionally at the image that I inadvertently projected at him.

"He's going to have to raise a heck of a lot more corpses in order to pull that off," Kala surmised. "Can you hack into the cameras around the cemeteries again?" she asked Mark.

"I'm way ahead of you," he replied and tapped the tablet that was nestled inside his jacket. "As soon as we've finished eating, we should head to the city so we can be there before the sun goes down."

Chapter Fifteen

As usual, Flynn stepped aside so I could climb into the SUV first. He waited until the car was in motion before he spoke. "If I were the bokor, I'd set up a ritual circle in several different cemeteries while it was still daylight. Once night fell, I'd move from one cemetery to the next, raising the zombies as quickly as I could."

Everyone turned to look at him with varying degrees of surprise. Reece contented himself with a glance into the rearview mirror. "Let's hope he doesn't figure that out," Mark said bleakly. He gestured at the cloudy sky as we neared the gate. "Thankfully, it's been raining all afternoon so any symbols that he's drawn would have been washed away by now."

"Not if he covered them over with something," Flynn countered. His expression became more animated as he thought the problem through. "Sheets of wood, tin or even plastic would do the trick. He'd just have to pile rocks on the corners to hold them in place so the circle wouldn't become smeared."

Kala was staring at him as if she'd never seen him before. "Am I the only one who is disturbed by how much thought you've put into this?"

He sent her a mock hurt look. "Hey, I'm just trying to anticipate the worst possible scenario."

Mark's frown deepened. "Believe me, you do not want to face the worst case scenario."

I had the feeling he'd been there and done that. "What would that be?" I asked.

"He could raise the wrong zombie and then we'd be in much more danger than just facing a young and inexperienced bokor."

"What kind of corpse is the wrong kind?" I persisted. The voodoo priestess had already given me a hint about this and I was interested in learning more.

"One that was a necromancer before they died," Reece answered flatly.

"Isn't necromancer just another name for a bokor?"

"No," Mark responded. "A bokor deals with spells, curses and dabbles in zombie raising. A necromancer's main talent is controlling the dead.

The practice largely died out a hundred years or so ago, thanks to the assistance of our organization."

I wished I'd had more time to read through the old PIA files. Knowledge of what we were facing would come in very handy. "I guess there are some necromancers buried in New Orleans?" I posed it as a question and both Mark and Reece nodded.

"Yes," Mark said. "A few notable souls have been interred in several of the cemeteries. I sincerely hope they remain in their crypts." A slight shudder went through him, which chilled me to the bone. He wasn't afraid of much, but he was clearly disturbed by this prospect.

"If the Zombie King did raise a necromancer, what would happen?"

"They'd be just a normal zombie to start with and the bokor wouldn't even be aware of the danger he was in," he said. "The problem begins once the necromancer feeds. Human blood revives all types of undead creatures." The only types of undead I knew about were zombies and vampires. I didn't even want to know what else was out there.

"With each meal that they consume, they become smarter and faster," he continued. "Necromancers have a natural affinity for the dead and when they're reanimated, they remember their past lives. They not only retain their ability to raise corpses, they actually become far better at it."

A heavy silence fell, but it didn't last long before Reece broke it. "I read a file about a necromancer that caused the deaths of hundreds of people in Germany a couple of hundred years ago." His tone was far too conversational for the topic that he was discussing. "A young witch stumbled across a spell that accidentally raised him from the dead. She wasn't able to control him and he killed her. He raised all of the dead in the cemetery and they ate their way through an entire village."

"I take it our predecessors stopped the necromancer and his undead friends," Kala said. Her normal exuberance was more subdued than usual.

"It was lucky that a member of our organization was visiting a relative in the next village," Mark said. "A survivor managed to flee and stumbled into the town seeking help. The villagers thought he was crazy at first, but some believed him. They formed a posse and waited for dawn when the zombies would be asleep. They found what was left of the bodies of their neighboring townsfolk dead inside their homes." I could easily picture a rustic little town with the gnawed bodies of people cast aside after the zombies were done with them.

"Zombies can't stand sunlight, but they don't burn up on contact like vampires do," he continued. "Our predecessor knew where they could be found and she made sure every dark place was searched. They dragged the undead out into the sunlight and set them on fire."

"I bet our establishment gained a few new members that day," Flynn said. It was impossible to pretend that monsters didn't exist once you became aware of them. I didn't know how the average person reacted to the news, but I certainly preferred to be proactive and take them down rather than hide under the bed. Then again, I was no longer average, or even completely human. To be perfectly honest, I enjoyed the hunt and I was looking forward to tracking the bokor down.

Mulling over Flynn's idea of setting up several circles during daylight hours, I wondered if the Zombie King would have the power to be able to resurrect his warriors in quick succession.

"He'd use up a lot of energy," Reece said in response to what should have been a private thought. "If the bokor were to try to raise zombies from multiple locations," he explained at the strange look Mark sent his way.

"He'll gain more power with practice," Mark said. "He's most likely been practicing on animals for the past few months or possibly even years."

Kala smirked. "It would have been a shock to his parents to see their pet cat or dog walking around after they'd been hit by a car."

"If he was devious enough, he'd have used his neighbors' pets to practice on," Flynn said.

Kala and I exchanged a look, then turned to him. "You almost sound as if you can identify with this guy," I said.

He shrugged, not even trying to look contrite. "I know what it's like to be young and cocky and to have abilities that few others have."

"But you don't bring things back from the dead," I said. "You just turn into a half-man, half-snake every now and then."

"Isn't that freaky enough?" he asked.

"Only if you start eating people," I responded. "Maybe then you could compare yourself to this guy."

He smiled and nudged me with his elbow, presumably in thanks for the moral support. The four of us might be supernatural creatures, but we weren't evil on the same level that our target was. We just lacked the ability to control our beasts when they rose, hence the thirty foot high fence that surrounded the entire compound.

A light drizzle settled in as we neared the city, making the road slick and hazardous and slowing traffic down. The sun disappeared behind the clouds and I wondered if that would have any effect on zombie raising. "Does it have to be full night before the bokor can raise his army?" I asked.

Mark inclined his head in response. "Even heavy cloud cover won't change that. The death magic is tied to nightfall. It can't be performed during daylight hours."

With every fact that I learned, I realized there was so much more that I didn't yet know. Agent Steel had been in this job since before my birth. I was beginning to think it would take me a very long time to learn enough to keep me alive.

We'd driven through and around New Orleans enough times by now for Reece to know the area well. He wended his way through the traffic to one of the cemeteries and we stepped out into the rain. The upside to the drizzle was that there were no tourists wandering around to interrupt us while we searched the boneyards.

We split up and I was paired with Kala while the others went their separate ways. We had the upper quadrant and kept our eyes out for symbols that had been drawn in blood. Kala spied something on the ground behind one of the larger crypts and we moved in for a closer look.

"Is that what I think it is?" I said incredulously when I saw the flat, square piece of bright blue tarpaulin. Four chunks of marble were holding it down.

"I hate it when Flynn's right," she muttered. "He has an uncanny knack for being able to get inside the target's heads sometimes."

We hunkered down and each lifted a corner of the plastic. Just as Flynn had predicted, the bokor had pre-drawn a circle in blood. It was slightly smeared from the tarp resting on it, but it was still intact.

"Did I just hear you say I was right?" Flynn asked, sounding pleased. We'd all switched on our earpieces after leaving the SUV so we could easily keep in touch.

"Yes," Kala replied with a long-suffering sigh. "What do you want us to do, boss?"

"Remove the plastic and let the rain wash the circle away," Mark said. "Once the diagram is broken, he'll have to redraw it."

I hadn't been able to sense anything because the zombies hadn't actually been called forth yet. This meant we'd have to search each cemetery for circles one by one. The sun would be down in an hour and we'd never get to them all in time.

Mark was already factoring this in and reached a decision. "We're going to have to split up and search all of the graveyards. Kala and Lexi, you stay on foot and take the four closest cemeteries to this one. I'll drop Reece and Flynn off on my way to search the others."

A surge of rebellion came through the bond a moment before Reece voiced his protest. "I don't think it's a good idea to leave the girls alone, sir."

"Excuse me?" Kala said in instant ire. "You think that our gender somehow makes us more vulnerable than you?" Her fists clenched and the veins in her forehead stood out. He'd pushed a button that had instantly enraged her.

"He means he doesn't want me out of Mark's sight," I said. What I really meant was that Reece didn't want me out of *his* sight. He trusted Kala with his life, but not with my safety.

"You think I can't protect Lexi better than Mark can?" she growled, un-mollified by my explanation.

"Do I need to remind you that I can rip a man in half with my bare hands?"

"We don't have time to argue about this," our boss cut in before the argument could escalate. "Alexis, are you happy to stay with Kala?"

Surprised that I was being given a choice, I responded immediately. "Of course. I trust her completely." That earned me a huge smile. Rain had plastered her tawny hair to her scalp and her mascara was running, but she still managed to look vivacious and pretty.

"You'd better keep her safe," Reece said just loudly enough for us shifters to hear him. His unspoken threat was that she'd be very sorry if anything happened to me.

Chapter Sixteen

Splitting up to search all of the cemeteries meant that we'd have to rely on our cell phones to keep in touch. I switched the tiny earpiece off and slipped it into my pocket. My white t-shirt and tan cargo pants were soaked all the way through from the steady rain. Normally, the extra weight of water would have slowed me down, but it did little to hamper my movements as I ran along the sidewalk beside Kala.

We left the graveyard, confident that the ritual circle had been rendered useless and headed for the next one that was only a few blocks away. The streets were largely deserted. Most people were smart enough to stay in out of the weather. Few cars passed us. We received strange stares from the occupants when they spied us jogging through the rain.

While we could have easily vaulted over the fence, we instead entered the next cemetery through the gate. Mark wasn't here to disable the CCTV cameras and we had to pretend to be just a normal pair of girls visiting a boneyard in the rain.

"We should split up," I said. "We'll get this done a lot quicker if we do."

"Garrett will kill me if he finds out I let you wander around alone."

Kala's tone was doubtful, but I could tell that she was in favor of the idea. "I'll be fine," I said and patted a bulging pocket on my pants. "I'm armed and I'm carrying enough ammo to kill half of the corpses in this place if they suddenly rise up and try to eat me."

"You have a point," she said with a grin and turned to search the left side while I made my way over to the other side.

We met at the top end of the cemetery when we'd finished scouring the place. My soggy companion lifted a brow in enquiry. "Did you find anything?"

I shook my head and water flew from the ends of my hair. The rain had picked up and had turned into a drenching downpour. "Nope. Let's head to the next cemetery before we lose the light." Not that nightfall would stop us, but even for us it would be more difficult to see the sheets of plastic in the dark.

Thankfully, she had a better sense of direction than I did and she knew exactly where the next stop on our list was. This boneyard was far larger and it was going to take us at least fifteen minutes to search it. We didn't even discuss staying together this time. Again, I took the right side and she took the left.

I finished my search before Kala and waited for her beneath an overhanging tree that offered at least some relief from the rain. If I'd been human, I'd have been shivering from the cold by now. To me, this was like a lukewarm shower but without the soap or shampoo.

A familiar sensation of being watched came over me. I turned in a slow circle, searching for whoever or whatever it was. Again, I felt someone foreign probing at my mind. The sensation grew stronger and stronger until if felt as if they were rushing towards me. A form loomed out of the darkness and I gasped in alarm.

"I found another circle and had to disable it," Kala said, not realizing that she'd come close to frightening the pants off me. The sensation of something dangerous approaching halted, then receded.

We only had about half an hour left before true nightfall now and we still had two cemeteries left to search, so we put on a burst of speed. "The last two graveyards are right across the street from each other," Kala said, as if she shared Reece's ability to read my mind. "You take the one on the right."

"Okay," I agreed and flicked a nervous glance upwards at the dark, cloudy sky. I couldn't feel any zombies anywhere nearby, but the bokor could turn up at any moment and call them from their slumber.

"Yell if you run into any trouble," she said before crossing the road. Our hearing was exceptional and we'd easily be able to hear each other if we shouted.

Tension seeped into my shoulders as I jogged up and down the rows of white marble crypts and dark gray mausoleums. I didn't see any sheets of plastic covering up bloody ritual circles. Even with the rain, I'd have been able to smell the blood. I returned to the road and met up with Kala again. The rain had eased off a few minutes ago and now it was just drizzling lightly.

"I'm kind of glad we didn't run into the Zombie King," she admitted. "Garrett would've torn me a new one if I'd let anything happen to you."

I was about to make a snide remark when my vision doubled and I was watching two different scenes at the same time. The alarm coming through the bond was a hint that the second image was coming from Reece. Closing my eyes to block out what was right in front of me, the bond showed me a young man with dark skin standing beside a freshly made circle of bloody symbols. He was dressed in black to better blend in with the shadows. His hands were raised and he was chanting in a foreign language.

"What's wrong?" Kala asked when I opened my eyes again, took her by the arm and started dragging her along the street.

"Reece is in trouble," I replied. It wasn't easy concentrating on where I was going while I was seeing two overlapping images.

Kala fumbled for her cell phone as I led the way through the now dark streets. Even the streetlights weren't doing much to combat the gloom. Part of me was watching where I was going, but the rest of my mind was with Reece. He lifted his gun to shoot, but we both knew he wasn't quite skilled enough to kill the target. He pulled the trigger and I heard the shot ring out through ears that didn't belong to me.

The Zombie King ducked as the bullet whizzed past him, missing him by only a few inches. He shouted a few last words to complete his spell and all hell broke loose. Zombies burst from their confinement and a green fog spread outwards with supernatural swiftness. It shrouded the cemetery and reduced visibility to only a few feet.

Reece felt compelled to rend and tear the walking corpses to pieces, but he was heavily outnumbered and common sense prevailed. I counted forty badly formed corpses shambling towards him before he turned and ran. It infuriated him to flee, but he was sensible enough to know that he couldn't take them all on by himself.

"Mark, Reece is under attack," Kala said when her call was answered.

"Why did he call you instead of me?" he asked, perturbed that he'd been left out of the loop.

"He, er, didn't call, exactly." She flicked a glance at me. "Lexi sensed that he was in trouble." I knew the others would find out that the bond between Reece and myself went both ways sooner or later. I'd hoped it would be much later than this.

"Call Flynn and tell him I'll pick him up. We'll meet you two there."

I was impressed with Kala's ability to dial and keep sprinting flat out without running into anything. It helped that she dropped back behind me and followed in my footsteps. "Mark's on his way to pick you up," she said as soon as Flynn answered. "The bokor sent a bunch of zombies after Garrett."

"You know this how?" he asked. I didn't need to see him to know he was alarmed that one of us was in trouble. I could hear it in his voice.

"I'll explain later," she said and hung up.

I didn't have time to feel guilty that I'd lied to the team about my ability to sense Reece. We were still several blocks away and the horde of undead was moving in to surround him. He'd managed to put a few of them down with headshots, but there were too many for him to kill on his own. The rain and eerie green fog weren't helping with his visibility. It would take skill and a natural ability to shoot to be able to hit the moving, half-seen monsters.

"Make sure I don't run into anything," I said and closed my eyes again.

"I don't know what you're planning to do, but I hope it works," she muttered as she slipped her arm through mine and guided me around the obstacles that I could no longer see.

Reece was momentarily startled when he felt me in his head far more strongly than ever before. This was the first time I'd actively tried to use the bond and it was disconcerting to us both. *Let me do the shooting,* I said directly into his mind.

Reluctant to relinquish control, he struggled with the idea of letting me take over. The decision was taken from him when two zombies lurched into view. Seizing control of a small part of his brain, I set his hands into motion. I sent three bullets into the first minion's left eye socket before it went down. It took five to kill the second one.

Automatically reaching into his pockets to grab fresh ammo, I ejected the magazine and rammed a new one home. I swiveled in time to take down a third slowly moving creature. Watching their comrades being cut down made the others more cautious, which meant they had a rudimentary intelligence. None had fed so far and they weren't really much of a threat yet. Once they tasted human flesh, they'd become far more of a danger.

Through the fog, I saw several more of the undead cautiously approaching. I blasted their heads apart before their milky eyes could latch onto Reece. Then the ground fell out from under me and my eyes snapped open.

"Sorry." Kala sent me an apologetic glance. "I should have warned you about the drop." We'd left the sidewalk to cross the street and I waited until we were back on the path before I closed my eyes again.

While I'd been distracted, Reece had moved to what he'd hoped would be a safer location. He'd chosen badly and he was now surrounded by the rotting carcasses of long dead people. His shots weren't as precise as mine and he gratefully allowed me to take over again. By now, Kala and I were close enough to hear the shots as I fired using his hands. I had a moment of dizziness at being in two places at once, then concentrated on the task at hand. Simply shooting out their eyes wasn't enough. They could still sense fresh meat and feel their way blindly towards him. Their brains had to be shredded with bullets before they'd go down and stay down.

"We're almost there," Kala told me. "Mark and Flynn just pulled up." I didn't open my eyes to see and trusted her to guide me into the cemetery. Twenty or so zombies were moving in, intent on feeding from Reece despite the number of fallen that surrounded him.

Opening my eyes when I was close enough to see the enemy, my gun was in my hand almost like magic and I blasted the skull of the closest zombie apart. Half of the malformed skeletons turned to face the new threat as we arrived, but the rest continued to lurch towards Reece. His expression was serene, but I felt his rage at being hunted by the disgusting abominations. I battled my instinctive fear and loathing as their slimy minds battered mine. I pumped round after round into them.

With five of us now blasting away at the minions, we quickly cut them all down, then took stock. All forty zombies lay on the ground. Shell casings littered the grass and concrete alongside them. Crypt lids had been either pushed aside or had been flung off completely with the zombies' escape. There was no sign of the bokor that had called the warriors from their graves. He'd wisely taken the opportunity to run.

"Does someone want to tell me what just happened?" Flynn asked. "How did you know Garrett was under attack?"

All eyes swung to me and I flushed beneath their scrutiny. "I lied when I said I couldn't sense him," I confessed.

"That went way beyond just sensing him," Kala said. "You were in his head helping him shoot, weren't you?"

Mark's astonishment was almost comical as he gaped at me. His soaked suit clung to him and he was shivering from the cold. "Is that true?"

"Do you think I managed to take them all down myself?" Reece asked dryly. "I'm good, but I'm not that good."

Our boss examined the bodies and saw that most of them had died from bullets through their eye sockets. I was the only one in the team who was capable of that kind of precision. "We three need to have a long talk about this," he decided.

A swell of power pulsed somewhere to the west and I turned to face it.

"What's wrong now?" Flynn asked almost wearily.

"The Zombie King just raised some more corpses," Reece answered for me. We were linked so strongly that it was a struggle to extricate myself from his mind.

Agent Steel wiped a hand over his dripping face and grimaced. "I still had one cemetery left to search. That must be where he is."

"It could have been worse," I reminded him. "We found two circles and managed to destroy them."

"I found two as well," Flynn said.

"I found this one a little too late," Reece put in.

"Lexi's right," Mark said. "It could have been much worse. We now have only one group of zombies left to destroy instead of six."

"How could he have the energy to raise so many minions in such a short space of time?" I asked as Mark pulled his cell phone out of his pocket.

"I doubt he'd have been able to utilize all of the circles," he said as he dialed the Cleanup Crew. "It was just dumb luck that he headed to the only other circle that we hadn't found."

After arranging for the Crew to take care of the mess that we'd left, Mark urged us towards the SUV. He'd used his electronic zapper to kill the cameras and this time he left them off so the Crew wouldn't be captured on tape. At least this cemetery was more isolated than the others and our shots had been mostly muffled by the persistent downpour. The cops hadn't been called by any concerned citizens. Our battle with the bokor would continue to rage beneath the noses of the citizens of New Orleans.

Chapter Seventeen

Mark had parked the SUV half a block away from the cemetery to avoid it being spotted by the cameras. The police would become suspicious if they saw our vehicle in the vicinity of the desecrations that were being made, or any further robberies that the bokor might stage. We had a legal right to investigate the crimes, but explaining who we were trying to apprehend would be difficult.

We climbed into the SUV and the seats instantly became soaked. While I was as bedraggled as Kala, at least I didn't have mascara running down my face. Mark handed her his dripping handkerchief. "You look like a raccoon," he explained at her quizzical look.

Most girls would have been insulted, but she just laughed. "That'll teach me to wear mascara in the rain." She wiped her face as clean as she could get it then turned to me. "Did I get it all?"

"Mostly," I replied and took the handkerchief. She sat patiently while I rubbed the rest away.

Flynn shook his head in disbelief when I handed the handkerchief back to Mark. "Why do girls have to be so vain?" he asked.

"Why do guys have to be so careless about their appearance?" Kala shot back. "If you spent more time on grooming maybe you'd pick up more often."

"I don't exactly live the kind of life where I can have a steady girlfriend," he retorted.

"Who said anything about a steady girlfriend? There's nothing wrong with a night or two of casual sex."

To me, there was plenty wrong with that. I just wasn't the type of girl who could trust someone that I didn't know with my body. Reece glanced into the rearview mirror and gave me a knowing look. My face flamed as I picked up the thought that I'd trusted him enough to sleep with him twice. The look faded when I silently reminded him that neither of us had had a choice about the incidents. Both times had literally been a life or death situation.

Mark's head swiveled from Reece to me and back again. He knew we were sharing something that the rest of them weren't privy to. Thankfully, he didn't demand to know what we were silently discussing.

It wasn't a long journey to the final cemetery, but we were too late to stop our quarry from completing his spell. The green fog that rose each time the reanimation ritual was used was already beginning to dissipate. I couldn't sense any zombies nearby and I could only feel the faint residue that they'd been here at all. "They're gone," I said before anyone could leave the SUV. "They went that way." I pointed up the street and Reece set the vehicle into motion without waiting for Mark's order.

I lost the trail after a few blocks and we cruised aimlessly in search of the truck and its unholy cargo of corpses. The bokor hadn't stuck around to rob another bank or to break into any other buildings. He was either exhausted after raising two separate groups of zombies, or he was afraid that we'd find him and shut him down. Personally, I thought the second option was more likely.

"Do you have any theories on what the Zombie King will do next?" I asked Flynn.

Unsure whether I was teasing him or not, he saw that I was serious and offered his opinion. "I think he's too arrogant to hide for long. Now that he knows he can raise two groups of zombies quickly, he'll probably try this again fairly soon. We can't be everywhere at once and he knows there are only a few of us. If I were him, I'd watch one of the cemeteries and move in when we finish searching it. He could raise his soldiers, squirrel them away then come back for more once or twice a night until he has all the puppets he needs."

"You'd make a really good bad guy," Kala leaned forward to say.

It was a backhanded compliment. "Thanks?" he said, unsure how to take it.

There was little point in driving around New Orleans now that the bokor had fled, so we returned to the compound. I stripped down and wrung the water out of my clothes as best I could before taking a shower. Dressing in a fresh t-shirt and comfortable sweatpants, I opened the door to find Mark standing on the other side and about to knock. He was carrying a basket full of soaked clothes. "Come with me," he ordered as I dumped mine on the top of the pile.

We stopped at the door three down from mine on the right and he balanced the basket on his hip and knocked. Reece opened the door dressed only in a pair of cutoff sweatpants. His expression was resigned when he saw us. He disappeared into his bathroom long enough to pick up his wet clothes and snagged a t-shirt from his dresser on the way back. Donning the shirt, he placed his wet clothing on top of mine then took the basket from Mark.

Taking the lead, Mark descended to the ground floor and we followed him down the long hallway to the laundry room. Our clothes went into the washing machine, then he escorted us to a meeting room just down the hall. The carpet was the same dark blue as the upstairs area and a long oval table took up most of the room. The last time we'd been in one of the conference rooms, I'd been given the shocking news that I was a werewolf. This time, we were here to discuss the bond that had been formed on the very night that I'd turned for the first time.

"Tell me about what happened between you tonight," Mark ordered and took a seat.

Reece sat across from him and I took the seat to his right. "I saw the bokor performing his ritual and knew I was too far away to hit him, but I took the shot anyway," he said. "I missed and he finished the spell and the zombies rose."

"I saw the danger as if I was looking through Reece's eyes," I explained. "I guess stress must have heightened our bond."

Nodding thoughtfully, Mark took his tablet out of his fresh suit and made a note on a file. "What happened next?"

Reece motioned for me to take over, so I explained how I'd spoken to him mind to mind and how I'd taken control of his hands. Mark's eyes widened at my description of using Reece to kill the zombies.

"I could have taken control back at any time," he said. "I thought it would be best to let Lexi take them down. She's a much better shot than me." It wasn't a compliment, but a simple fact.

"I've never heard of this happening before," Mark said. He made a few more notes, then slid the tablet back into his pocket. "I wish I knew what was so special about you two." He frowned and studied us both. "It will be interesting to see how this develops."

"I don't know about you, but I could really use a cup of coffee," I said, hoping to deflect the conversation to a safer topic.

Mark checked his watch with a frown. "Isn't it a little late for coffee?" It was nearing two o-clock and we'd be getting up in a few hours.

"Nope," I replied. "I'm already wired and I doubt the caffeine will affect me much more."

He might be my boss, but he wasn't my parent and Mark kept his concerns to himself. "Don't stay up too late," he warned me as he stood.

"Yes, Mom," Reece murmured just loudly enough for me to hear him and I coughed to hide my snigger.

Shooting a suspicious glance at us over his shoulder, Mark shook his head and let himself out into the hallway. He turned right to check on our clothes and I turned left. Reece was on my heels when I reached the door to the main area. I was surprised when he followed me into the kitchen and watched me switch on the coffee machine. He shook his head when I lifted a mug, silently enquiring if he wanted a drink.

"I just wanted to thank you for saving my butt," he said. "It was weird having you inside my head, but if you hadn't taken over, I'd probably be dead." It was said in a matter-of-fact tone and my heart clenched at how close I'd come to losing him.

"You'd have done the same for me," I said awkwardly, unused to the praise.

"Let's hope I never have to," he replied then loped towards the stairs. I watched him climb the spiral staircase two at a time wistfully. His thanks had been sincere, but beneath it I'd sensed his unhappiness that I'd been able to take control of even a small part of him. Flynn's theory that Reece's wolf didn't want to be alone might be true, but his human side sure wasn't happy about being lumped with me.

Chapter Eighteen

Flynn's prediction that the bokor would act sooner rather than later turned out to be wrong. Five nights passed before he finally came out of hiding. He was correct when he'd guessed that the Zombie King would lie in wait for us to search one of the cemeteries before moving in to perform his ritual again.

After four afternoons and nights of fruitlessly searching the cemeteries for ritual circles, I was frankly getting bored. Mark had paired me up with Flynn this time and we were watching one of the graveyards from a café across the street. It was another rainy night and I held a steaming mug of coffee in both hands.

Two young women were sitting at a table across the room and were sending flirtatious looks at my companion. He ignored them both, but he was well aware of their scrutiny. "You know, either one of those girls would be happy to go out with you," I said quietly.

Sending me a startled glance, his eyes slid sideways to examine the pair. "They're pretty, but I'm not interested."

"Why not?" I asked him bluntly.

"What would be the point?" he shrugged. "We're only going to be in New Orleans until our mission is over. Then we'll head back to Denver until we're needed somewhere else."

"You're not into one night stands?" I teased.

"I'm not Kala," he responded. "She might be the love them and leave them type, but that just isn't me."

"Is that because of your inner snake or is that just you?"

He shrugged again and picked up his coffee. "I don't know," he said honestly. "I was injected with the virus when I was a toddler. I have no way of knowing what I would have been like if I was still human."

I had changed in some ways, but I was still me on the inside. "For what it's worth, I don't think our morals change when we become shifters," I told him. "I still feel the same way towards relationships as I did before I was bitten."

His weird green eyes studied me closely. "What is your policy about dating?"

"It was never that important to me. I'd intended to put my career first," I said softly and stared out the window into the drizzle. "It sounds corny, but I figured that I'd eventually meet the right man when I was ready to settle down."

"You'd buy a house in the suburbs, raise two or three kids and have a normal life together," he said with a nod of understanding.

Sadness rose when I realized none of that would ever happen now. I hadn't just lost my dream career when I'd become a shifter. I'd also lost any hope of having a family. Being bonded to Reece meant that there would be no children for me now. I'd never allow myself to fall pregnant to a man who could barely tolerate my presence.

Blinking back tears, I had to put my misery and self-pity on hold when I felt a swell of power.

Flynn picked up on my tension immediately. "Is it the bokor?" he leaned in to ask in a low voice and I nodded. He took his cell phone out and dialed Mark. "The Zombie King is up to his old tricks," he said without preamble.

"Where?" Agent Steel asked.

"Somewhere to the south," I said to Flynn and he repeated my directions.

"I'll pick you up in five minutes."

Quickly draining our coffee, we left the café and stood beneath an awning as we waited for the SUV to appear. We detoured to pick up Reece and Kala before speeding towards the area where I'd sensed the latest batch of zombies being cooked.

"They're still here," I said as we closed in on the graveyard. I could still feel the undead milling around inside the fog-shrouded place.

"Grab the flamethrowers," Mark ordered as he pulled to a stop. We weren't isolated enough to be able to use our guns this time and it wasn't raining quite heavily enough to douse the flames.

"Lexi, stay with me," he said. "We'll enter from the south. Reece, take the north." Reece nodded and peeled off even before Mark finished. "Kala, you have the west. Flynn, you take the east. If you see the Zombie King, take him down," he ordered. Now that his minions had fed on human flesh, we wouldn't detain our target. He'd been bumped up from an annoyance into an outright danger and had signed his own death warrant.

Mark zapped the cameras and we hurried through the gate and entered the smallish cemetery. This time there were only thirty or so corpses gathered together. I didn't see a human hiding among them.

We waited for the others to shift into position before we moved in closer. The zombies sensed me when we were about twenty feet away and turned to attack. Slow and stupid, they were no match for our flamethrowers. We turned them into charred lumps of flesh in mere minutes.

Kala nudged a smoldering corpse with her boot and made a face when it broke apart. "Why do I get the feeling these zombies were just a distraction?"

Mark's phone rang and he fished it out of his jacket. "This is Agent Steel." He listened intently and we all heard his contact advising him that a jewelry store had been broken into a few minutes ago. Tens of thousands of dollars' worth of merchandize had been taken.

"Thanks for the update," he said when his contact finished giving him his report.

"You didn't see that coming," Kala complained to Flynn.

"Actually," he argued, "I figured he'd use some of his zombies as a decoy sooner or later."

"We can't predict exactly what the bokor is going to do every time," Mark said wearily as he dialed the Cleanup Crew. "We can only do our best."

Unfortunately, our best wasn't good enough. The Zombie King kept eluding us and we were starting to look like amateurs. The glimpse I'd caught of him through Reece hinted that he was fairly young. How could he be so damn wily?

Leaving the mess for the Crew to deal with, we hastened back to the SUV to investigate the jewelry store. The same two cops that had turned up to the bank robbery were standing on the sidewalk when we drove past. The younger cop glared at us suspiciously, but the windows were too heavily tinted for him to see inside. Something about his pale eyes gave me the creeps. To add to my heebie-jeebies, the unseen watcher was back again. Picking up on my unease, Reece watched me from time to time as he made a circuit of the city.

"I doubt the bokor will strike again tonight," Mark decided after we'd been driving around for a couple of hours in search of him.

"He's probably hiding in his lair playing with his treasure," Flynn agreed darkly.

"I bet he's laughing at us right now," Kala said. Her arms were crossed and her expression was belligerent. Her short, golden blond hair was spiky from running her hands through it in frustration.

We arrived back at the compound at a decent hour this time. After taking a shower, I carried my laptop downstairs to the living room. Kala and Flynn were watching a movie about werewolves. They howled in laughter each time an error about our kind was made. Neither of them turned into wolves, but they shared the same general traits as Reece and me. We were all allergic to silver, but some of the items that were supposed to either kill or incapacitate us were ludicrous. How could roses possibly harm us, I wondered as I flicked a glance at the screen.

Ignoring them both as well as I could, I searched the PIA files for bokors and voodoo practitioners. After a couple of hours of reading and two cups of coffee, I hadn't learned anything new.

The next search I ran was for necromancers. One account had been recorded just before the Civil War by an early member of the organization. A slave had murdered a plantation owner and had resurrected him. He'd been so skilled that the dead man had passed as being alive for six months before the deception had finally been discovered. Every single slave on the property had been slaughtered in retaliation by the authorities.

There were a few more accounts, but only one story of a necromancer that had died and had then been reanimated. The episode had occurred just over a century ago and a photo had been taken by a PIA operative. Sepia toned, the photo was grainy, yet chilling. A zombie stared back at the camera with intelligence burning in its slightly milky eyes. It had fed well and was in much better shape than any of the living dead that I'd seen so far.

Kala leaned over to look at the screen and wrinkled her nose. "He's a handsome guy," she said sarcastically.

"He's a zombie necromancer," I said.

Flynn left his seat and came to sit on my other side. He leaned in to take a look as well and I was boxed in by them both.

"What does the file say about him?" the blond agent asked.

I opened the file and we read through it together. The necromancer had been resurrected by his widow. He'd taught her how to raise zombies and they'd made a pact to bring each other back if either of them died. They hadn't taken into account the fact that their affection for each other would die with them. While their bodies could be resurrected, love couldn't be revived. She'd been able to control him until he'd first fed. Then he'd promptly turned on her and had killed her.

"That's true love for you," Flynn said as he read the last paragraph. He read almost as slowly as me.

"He ate her heart." Kala's tone was incredulous and disgusted. "Do zombies usually do that?"

"Just the ones that were necromancers when they were alive," Reece said as he descended the stairs and loped towards the kitchen. I flicked a glance over my shoulder to see him wearing only a pair of jeans that rode down low on his hips.

"How do you know so much about them?" I asked.

"I've read through most of the PIA files," he said.

Kala held up her empty mug. "I'll have one," she said by way of a request.

Reece beckoned with his hand and she tossed the mug to him. His bicep flexed as he snagged it out of the air one handed. He caught the mug that Flynn threw at him a second later. He lifted his eyebrow at me and it was my turn to toss him my cup. My aim was slightly off and he reached out to snag it before it hit the wall.

"Looks like we'll have to teach you how to throw as well as fight," he said with a hint of a grin.

Kala elbowed me in the side to snap me out of my stare. Would I ever get used to seeing him half clothed?

"If you say anything about eye candy, I'll shoot you," I said in a low voice.

"Ooh," she said in mock fright. "I'm so scared!"

"I would be if I were you," Flynn said, half seriously. "Did you see what she did to those zombies?" He slouched back and put his arm along the back of the couch, which brought him into contact with my shoulder. He didn't mean anything by it, but Reece inadvertently sent a flare of jealousy at me anyway. "How did you manage to shoot them all in the eye like that? It was so dark and foggy that you should have barely been able to see them."

"Don't forget that Lexi was using my eyes and hands rather than her own, which would have made it that much harder," Reece said as he carried four mugs into the living room.

He handed the drinks out and took a seat beside Kala. It was rare for us all to sit and relax together, but we'd earned the break. Mark was in the coms room, engrossed with the computer.

"What does it feel like when you're in each other's heads?" Kala asked almost hesitantly, as if expecting us to be angry at being questioned.

Reece leaned forward to meet my eyes and we both shrugged. "It's hard to explain," he replied. "I can always feel her in there, but I can smother the link if I try hard enough. I get this strange tingle in the back of my head when she's trying to contact me."

That was the same sensation I felt when I was close to the zombies or the unknown watcher that was apparently stalking me. It was highly disturbing that I was able to feel things that no one else could. It had to have something to do with the battle that was supposedly going on inside me. I wished I could just be normal. Or as normal as a creature like me could possibly be.

"What was it like when Lexi took over and started shooting the zombies?" Flynn asked.

"It was highly…intense," Reece replied. That wasn't the word he'd been going to use, but it was close. The actual word had been 'intimate' and it was fitting. Our minds had melded tightly together. I had the feeling that if we'd wanted to, we could have rifled through each other's thoughts and learned anything that we'd wanted to know.

"Can you take Lexi over like that?" Kala wanted to know and dread seized me when Reece leaned forward to look at me again.

"I don't know," he said, sensing my reluctance to be a lab rat for our friends.

Flynn made a point that I wished he'd kept to himself. "It's only fair if you can test to see if it goes both ways."

Kala nodded in agreement. "That's true."

Giving in to the inevitable, I shrugged and handed my laptop to Flynn. "Just don't make me cluck like a chicken," I said to Reece.

A look of concentration came over him then his eyes closed and I felt him invade my mind. I instinctively shut down my thoughts to keep him out and only allowed him the same control he'd given to me. "He's in my head and is seeing through my eyes," I told our team mates as my vision doubled for a moment before becoming clear again. I looked down at my hands and they seemed unusually small.

Kala edged forward so she could see Reece's face to make sure his eyes were closed and held up her hand. "How many fingers am I holding up?"

"Three," he responded immediately. "Nice," he said dryly when she curled two of her fingers down so only the middle one was left. "Very ladylike."

She giggled and then it was Flynn's turn to make a request. "Can you make Lexi pick up her mug?" Flynn queried.

Feeling like a puppet, I didn't fight it as Reece reached out to grab the steaming mug. He lifted it to my mouth and I took a sip and swallowed. His eyes flew open in shock. "I could taste that!"

Mark had descended the stairs and overheard his statement. "Your bond must be even stronger than I'd anticipated," he mused as he joined us on the couch. "I'd like to explore this further." I tried to hide my scowl behind my mug, but he saw it anyway. "Don't you want to learn as much about your bond as possible?"

"Not really," I replied. "I'd rather just get rid of it entirely."

Strangely, that inflicted a stab of hurt on Reece. He squelched the emotion and I pretended that I hadn't felt it at all. Didn't he want to be free? Surely he didn't want to be shackled to me for the rest of his life.

Chapter Nineteen

After a day spent training with the team and a solid two hours of sparring with Reece to learn how to control my anger, I was feeling edgy. He'd pushed me harder than usual, bringing my rage to the surface then forcing me to quell it again and again. Was this punishment for hurting his feelings? I thought women were supposed to be complicated, but his moods were just as hard to decipher as ours.

Leaving the compound in mid-afternoon, we performed another fruitless search of all fifteen cemeteries, then took a break before the sun went down. We ordered fast food and took it to a nearby park. The sky was clear and nightfall wasn't far away. Smells washed over us continually and I'd already learned to tune most of them out. Then the breeze wafted a different scent over and I wasn't the only one to turn and stare at the street.

"What is it?" Mark asked with his mouth full of fries.

Kala smirked, but refrained from making a snide remark about talking with his mouth full. "We just smelled the bokor." We'd all picked up his scent after we'd rescued Reece from death by zombie horde.

"He isn't in the truck this time," Flynn said. He was facing the street and had been watching the traffic pass by.

The bokor didn't have his minions with him, which meant he was most likely going to create some more. "Is anyone else getting sick of driving around hoping we'll stumble across him?" I complained.

"Yes," our boss replied, surprising us all. "But what choice do we have? He's becoming more skilled with practice and he can now raise a large number of zombies in just a few minutes. If we had help, we could watch all of the cemeteries at once. With only five of us, the odds aren't good."

"What if each of us stakes out a cemetery and you hack into the CCTV cameras that are around the other ten?" Kala asked. "You can buy us all a tablet and we can all watch three graveyards at once," she proposed. "Even if we don't see the bokor in action, the green fog should show up on our screens when he raises his next batch of undead. We can head there as soon as we spot it and have a better chance of catching him."

Mark turned to her in astonishment. "That's an excellent idea, Agent Walker."

"You're not going to leave Alexis alone in a graveyard with a powerful bokor on the loose?" Reece said in disbelief that our boss was even contemplating the idea.

"Who saved who's butt again?" I said mildly, reminding him of just how many zombies I'd taken out with his hands and eyes.

"We can't treat her like a baby forever," Flynn said. "Lexi is smart and capable. She can handle herself." I grinned to show my appreciation of his support even if I did feel a little nervous at the idea of being on my own. I hadn't forgotten the unknown watcher that was stalking me like a shark circling its prey.

Mark checked his watch and motioned for us to finish our meals quickly. "The stores should still be open. Let's get a move on." He used his tablet to search for the closest electronic store that stocked the items we needed while the rest of us finished our meals.

We piled into the SUV and made our way to the store. We waited in the car while Mark made his purchases. He returned after a few minutes and spent some time linking all five tablets together. I had no idea how he did it, but he set the tablets to watching two different cemeteries each. When he was done, he handed them over to us. I'd been assigned three of the graveyards that Kala and I had searched together. They were close together and it would take less than five minutes to sprint to the two that were displayed on my monitor if I spied the bokor in action.

Mark was much slower on foot than any of us so he'd take the SUV. I was the first to be dropped off and Flynn climbed out to let me disembark from the vehicle. Mark turned to face me before I made it to the door. "Call me if you see the bokor, or if you feel you're in any danger."

Reece turned his head slightly and watched me from the corner of his eye. I caught his thought that I should reach out to him as well and nodded to them both. "Yes, sir."

With the tablet tucked beneath my arm, I headed to the cemetery and performed a thorough search. There were no new circles drawn on the ground and no signs that any of the crypts or mausoleums had been disturbed since we'd last searched the place.

Full dark descended and the reality of my current location hit me. I was alone in an ancient cemetery. I'd never been particularly afraid of the dark before, but I couldn't deny the smidgeon of fear that crept over me now.

Climbing up onto one of the crypts, I sat with my legs crossed and settled down to watch the tablet. After an hour or so, my butt went to sleep and I climbed down to stretch my legs. My cell phone rang and I fumbled it out of my pocket to see that Mark was calling.

"I'm just checking in," he said when I answered the phone. "Have you seen or sensed anything yet?"

I was about to answer in the negative, but hesitated when the insidious feeling that I was being watched crept over me again. "Nothing so far," I replied. For all I knew, the sensation was just in my mind.

"I'll keep in touch every hour, unless one of us spots the bokor," he promised, then hung up.

Pretending that I wasn't aware I was being scrutinized, I walked up and down the row of crypts, keeping a close watch on the tablet. I'd expected the Zombie King to have made his move by now, but there had been no sign of him yet.

Close to the second hour of waiting, I was bored out of my mind. A casual glance around made me freeze for a moment as I spied someone standing in the shadows of a mausoleum several rows away. Even with my heightened eyesight, they were just a vague outline.

My cell phone rang again and I looked away from the shadowy figure to answer it. When I looked again, they were gone and so was the sensation of being watched. "Hi, Mark," I said, trying to keep my voice even.

"We're on our way to pick you up," he said. "It seems the bokor has a different plan in mind tonight. We'll be there in five minutes." He didn't elaborate further.

I was the last one to be picked up. Kala opened her door and motioned for me to climb over her. I scrambled inside and we took off even before I was seated. The blond agent let out a startled sound when

I landed in her lap. "Sorry, Lexi, you're pretty and everything but you're really not my type," she said.

Flynn laughed and took my hand to haul me into the middle seat. Even Reece was smiling. Mark and I weren't anywhere near as amused as them. I rested the tablet on my lap and braced myself as best I could as we took a corner way too fast.

"Where are we headed?" I asked when my heart dislodged from my throat enough for me to speak. It had been a while since I'd been disturbed by our chauffeur's maniacal driving skills.

"I was randomly checking the CCTV cameras around the city when I spied green fog coming from a retirement home a few minutes ago," Mark replied. "We're on our way to investigate it now."

"I have a bad feeling about this," Flynn said in dread at what we'd find when we arrived. I shared his trepidation.

Speeding as much as he dared, Reece soon eased to a halt outside a decrepit old house. A worn sign that read 'Shady Rest Retirement Home' was the only indication that it wasn't just another old, rundown home in desperate need of a makeover.

Green fog spilled from the open front door and the sounds of chewing came from within. "Do you hear that?" I whispered to the others with a sick feeling in my stomach.

"What is it?" Mark asked quietly.

"The zombies are feeding," Reece said bleakly.

Mark's face turned even more somber. We each took a flamethrower from the back of the SUV then moved into a huddle. "Reece and Flynn, take the back. Girls, you're with me. There's a good chance that the bokor is still inside and I don't want to give him an opportunity to escape."

We gave the guys enough time to sprint to the back of the house, then Kala used her foot to push the front door open wider. A body lay on the floor just inside the door. It was a female and she had white, wispy hair and thin, papery skin. Her nightgown was torn open and her innards had been eaten. Her expression was frozen in pain and terror. If this had been a horror movie, she'd have turned into one of the things that had eaten her by now. Since it was a bokor that had raised the zombies, she'd stay dead unless he worked his dark magic to add her to his growing army.

The chewing sounds were coming from deeper inside the retirement home. We crept down a long hallway, stepping over three more bodies. Rooms branched off to either side, but there was no one dead or alive inside any of them.

At the back of the house, we reached a large open area where the residents gathered for their recreation time. Twenty or so zombies were hunkered over the bloody corpses of their fellow elderly. I caught a hint of movement and glanced beyond the feeding creatures to see the bokor watching us in shocked surprise.

"He didn't think we'd be able to find him," Kala said in satisfaction.

The Zombie King gave an order to his freshly made minions. "Protect me!" he screamed.

In a blur of motion, I pulled my gun from my pocket and aimed. Moving almost as fast as me, the zombies stood, ruining my shot. The bokor fled before I could fire, then I was busy trying to stay alive. Unlike the previous undead that we'd faced, these ones were faster and were far more alert. I wasn't sure if their alertness was because they were freshly dead rather than long dead, or if it was due to their recent meal.

Fire flared and the zombies let out buzzing cries of pain as their clothes ignited. They were harder to kill than the older, far less well maintained undead, but they eventually went down. Simply calling the Cleanup Crew in to dispose of the bodies wasn't going to work this time. Questions would be asked that couldn't easily be answered. It didn't take an expert to see the knife wounds in the roasted corpses. The bokor had crept inside the retirement home and had snuck from bed to bed, slashing the throats of half of the inhabitants before raising them. The other occupants of the home had been used as food for his newly raised minions.

"This guy is seriously sick," Flynn said, looking ill.

"He must have thought that using fresh dead would be a better idea than resurrecting old corpses," Mark responded.

Kala hesitated, then her mischievousness took over. "Well, they're not exactly *young* corpses, are they? Technically, they were already pretty old before he killed them and turned them into zombies."

Mark sent her a withering stare, then called the Cleanup Crew in. This time, we stayed until the pair arrived. Taking in the state of the bodies, the team of two huddled together with Mark to decide the best way to handle this.

Reaching their decision, our boss called us over. "Help us put them all back in their beds," he said. "We're going to burn the place to the ground. I'll make a call to my superiors and ask them to smooth things over with the local authorities so they don't ask too many questions."

From the sounds of it, he'd used this tactic before with success. The retirement home was enclosed by a large yard on all sides. It should be isolated enough not to set the buildings on either side alight.

I wasn't happy about lugging either the eaten corpses or the dead zombies around, but kept my complaints to myself. While I felt no pity or remorse for killing our targets, I did feel compassion for the poor old people who'd died this night. Instead of living out the remainder of their lives in tranquility, they'd been brutally murdered and their bodies had been defiled. It was distressing to realize that even in death, sometimes there was no peace.

Following my fellow agents' example, I tucked two bodies beneath my arms at a time and carried them to the bedrooms upstairs. It was easy enough to work out which body belonged in which bed. Their scents were clear enough and led us to the correct rooms. We had more trouble with the charred zombies, but eventually we had everyone in their proper places.

A few of the dead were much younger and must have been the live-in staff. We placed them into their beds on the second floor as well, then Mark used his flamethrower to start a fire at the back of the building. The Cleanup Crew tossed an accelerant on the flames and the fire took off. They splashed more of the liquid in each room and Mark used his flamethrower to ignite more beds with their already dead occupants.

We worked our way down to the ground floor where the Crew splashed more of the fluid around. Moving quickly, Mark shot a final burst of flame then we vacated the house. Both the van and our SUV took off as sirens wailed and rapidly drew closer. The dark blue sedan with the two cops that had investigated the bank robbery and jewelry store heist sped past us. They were moving too fast to take note of our vehicle or else they may have turned around to follow us.

"I can't believe the bokor got away again," Kala grumbled. "He must have the luck of the devil."

"That was my fault," I admitted. "I should have moved faster."

Mark turned and frowned at my dejected tone. "I don't think it's humanly possible for you to have moved any faster than you did."

I'd been quick to draw my weapon, but not quick enough. "But I'm not human," I reminded him glumly.

"We'll get him eventually," Reece said. "He'll make a mistake and we'll be there to stop him." I wished I had his confidence that we'd be able to put a stop to this monster before he took any more lives.

Chapter Twenty

I watched the local news on the TV in my bedroom when I woke the next morning. The fire at the retirement home was the top story. It had been ruled as a tragic accident due to faulty wiring and inadequate smoke alarms. No mention was made of knife wounds, missing organs, or teeth marks on any of the remains. Mark's superiors had pulled enough strings to ensure that the Zombie King and his undead warriors remained beneath the radar. Sooner or later, the cops would stumble across our target first. When that happened, there would be no way to keep the supernatural elements secret.

Musing about this over breakfast, I turned to ask Mark a question to find him watching me. "Is something on your mind?" he asked.

"What happens if the police catch the bokor in the act of raising, or using his zombies?"

"They'll most likely die."

I already knew that, but that wasn't what I was asking. "What if they don't die? What if we swoop in and save them after they've already seen the undead walking around?"

Reece knew where I was going with this line of enquiry. "Lexi wants to know if we'll kill the cops to keep them silent."

"Oh." Mark looked down at his toast and frowned. It wasn't a good sign that he was having trouble meeting my eyes.

"We wouldn't, would we?" I was appalled at the idea. "We're supposed to track and kill the bad guys, not innocent cops who are just doing their jobs."

"Killing them would be a last resort," Agent Steel said, now toying with his cup of coffee.

I caught a fleeting thought from Reece and turned to him. "You use mind control?" I asked. "Are you saying that we can wipe their memories?"

"Not us," Kala replied to my incredulous query. "We'd have to call in the Sweepers for that."

I groaned and put my hands over my face. "Sweepers?" It came out muffled.

"Mind Sweepers," Flynn clarified. "They're experts at using a blend of chemicals and a form of brain washing to tweak the memories of anyone who learns about the supernatural world."

Dropping my hands, I pushed away my mostly empty bowl. "Is there anything else about the PIA that I don't know about?"

Mark's smile was strained. "Of course. There are branches of the PIA that even I'm not aware of. We all have different clearance levels and we're trusted with only a certain amount of information."

"What's my clearance level?" I asked.

Kala smirked and answered me before Mark could. "You're still basically a trainee. You have the lowest clearance. You're lucky we tell you anything."

Mark shot her a dark look and answered me more seriously. "There are ten levels. You're at level one. I'm at level eight."

"What about you guys?" I pointed at the other shifters.

"We're at level five," Flynn said. "We know enough to do our jobs and to know what kind of creatures are out there, but we don't know enough to be a liability if we're ever compromised."

His answer confused me more than it helped me. "Do I even want to know what you mean by that?"

Slumped back in his chair and stretched his legs out, Reece's bare foot bumped into mine, which sent a small spark through us both. Even the smallest contact of skin to skin affected us. "We're not the only organization that is aware of the supernatural world," he said.

A sneaking suspicion hit me and I sent Mark an accusing glare. "You lied to me about who captured your team when they were toddlers. They weren't rogue scientists at all, were they? They belonged to the same kind of institute as the PIA."

He shook his head and lifted his shoulders. "I told you as much of the truth as I was able, Alexis."

His tone was disapproving and I realized that I'd crossed the line. "I shouldn't have questioned you," I apologized immediately. My father had taught me to treat my elders with more respect than that. "It's just hard to realize how little I know about all this." I waved my hand to encompass the wide range of information that I wasn't yet privy to.

He inclined his head in acceptance of my apology. "I don't blame you for being annoyed at being kept in the dark. In time, you'll have the same level of knowledge as the rest of the team."

"If you read through the PIA files, you'll learn more than Kala and Flynn know now," Reece pointed out. "You won't have access to all the files, but enough of it to learn what you need."

Kala and Flynn scowled in unison. "Reading through the files is boring," Kala whined.

"We have better things to do with our time," Flynn agreed.

"I like reading through cases that are three or four hundred years old," I said to their mutual disgust. "It's interesting," I insisted.

"Sure it is," the blond agent said with an exaggerated eye roll. "It's about as interesting as baking a cake." After her one and only failed attempt at baking, that had to mean she really hated reading through the files.

"Getting back to your original question," Mark said before we could become distracted from the topic at hand. "If any civilians or police officers learn the truth, I'll call in the Mind Sweepers and they'll work their magic to wipe away any memories of zombies."

Mollified by his answer, I nodded gratefully. The thought of murdering humans just because they'd seen what we deal with in our line of work every day didn't sit well with me. It occurred to me that my father was lucky that his memory hadn't been wiped. I wasn't entirely certain how much he knew about the paranormal world, but he knew what I'd become.

If he and Mark hadn't been friends, would he have been told that I'd died rather than the truth? I felt a stab of grief that he'd have lived out the rest of his life thinking that he was alone. Reece picked up my emotion and looked at me uncertainly. I was working on masking the bond and clamped down harder. Frowning at being shut out, he stood to take care of his dishes.

"Who were the people that changed you all into shifters?" I asked. Mark had basically admitted to me that he'd killed the people responsible.

"I'm afraid we can't tell you that," he said. "Just the fact that you're aware that another organization exists is above your clearance level."

Something in his expression told me that he wanted to tell me, but couldn't. Maybe reading through the archives would tell me what I wanted to know. "Never mind. I'll just wait until I have the proper clearance then."

Our close encounter with our target had frightened the bokor enough that he laid low for the next few days. I could feel the power of the moon growing with each night that passed. If the voodoo priestess knew who and what we were, then it was possible that the bokor was also aware. He could be biding his time, planning on unleashing his servants when we were locked away in our enclosures. If so, then there was nothing we could do to stop him.

Mark held a meeting on the morning of the full moon. We gathered around the dining table and the room crackled with suppressed energy. I could barely sit still and felt the urge to kick off my shoes and to sprint through the marshy woods at the back of the compound. It was difficult to concentrate on the speech that he was making, but I forced myself to listen.

"I'll keep watch over the cemeteries and do my best to track the bokor while you four are occupied for the next three nights," he said.

"What if he robs another bank, or targets another retirement home while we're in our were-forms?" Kala asked.

Mark shrugged, but his expression was worried. "There's nothing we can do about that. We'll just have to wait for the full moon to wane, then resume our mission again."

It was a short speech and he released us to our own devices. It was impossible to try reading through the archives when I couldn't even sit still for five minutes at a time. I spent the day learning how to wrestle with Kala and Flynn rather than training with knives or sticks. They had very different styles and it was interesting to learn from them both. I quickly learned that I was much weaker than them. I'd have to build up my strength to have a chance at holding my own in the ring.

Training all day should have worn me out, but I was still full of energy when the sun began to sink from the sky.

We called a halt to wrestling just before dark and went our separate ways. Kala's room was next to mine and she spoke to me before opening her door. "I wouldn't bother eating dinner tonight," she warned me. "You'll be chasing down and devouring anything that moves as soon as the moon comes up." Pushing her door open, she stepped inside, then stuck her head back out as another thought occurred to her. "You should pack a bag with a change of clothes so you'll have something fresh to wear when you're human again. You might want to wrap a plastic bag around it to keep the rain out."

"Thanks for the tip," I said and she grinned, then disappeared from view.

I found an old backpack that someone had left in the closet and put a change of clothes inside. There would be no need to take any weapons with me. I'd be the deadliest thing in the prison that had been created just for me.

Mark met me in the hallway when I left my bedroom. "The others have gone on ahead," he told me. "I thought I'd escort you to your enclosure."

"Thanks." His offer touched me more than I could express. He wasn't going to let me face my second change alone, even if he could only take me as far as the gate.

We traipsed downstairs, then took the long hallway to the exit that led to the grounds behind the compound. The boundaries of the existing enclosures had been shifted to create my prison, which meant the hunting grounds had been reduced for everyone. It wasn't an ideal situation, but there hadn't been enough time to create an entirely new enclosure for me.

We walked to the far edge of the gun range and followed a narrow path through the trees. The silver fence came into view and we walked over to a newly made gate. My prison was between Reece's and Flynn's enclosures. Mark had turned the electricity off so the fence was safe, but instinct warned me to stay away from it. So did the dead dove that was rotting on the ground a few yards away.

Mark checked his watch, looked up at the dark sky, then gestured at the scanner that had been erected next to the fence. "You'd better go in. The moon will rise soon."

I didn't need his warning to know that the change was about to happen. The beast inside me wanted out and I could almost feel it panting in the back of my head. "I'll see you in three days," I said flippantly and swallowed down my nervousness. I sensed Reece nearby, but he was too far back in the trees for me to see him. He guarded his thoughts, but I sensed his excitement about being able to unleash his wolf.

"Stay safe," Agent Steel said softly as I placed my hand on the scanner and the gate clicked open.

"Always," I replied and loped away from the fence as he pulled the gate shut.

I didn't have to go far before I was swallowed up by trees. Listening hard, I couldn't hear Reece or Flynn. Even with our keen eyesight, I was too deeply within the enclosure for either of them to be able to see me. This was as private as I was going to get.

Nocturnal animals and birds mostly ignored me as I stripped down to my skin. A breeze lifted my hair, but it did nothing to cool me down. Even though I knew what was happening to me this time, I was still frightened by the transformation that I was about to undergo once again. My breath came faster and faster as the moon brightened and rose higher in the sky.

Moments before pain exploded through my body, Reece reached out and touched my mind. I latched onto him in desperation as the beast took control. Screams issued from my throat as my bones were broken down and were remade into my new form. Fur sprouted all over my body and I fell forward onto my hands and knees. Claws replaced my fingernails and dug into the dirt as agony spread through me.

It happened much quicker this time, but it was no less painful. I gnashed the air with my fangs as my jaw lengthened, then threw my head back and howled as the transformation came to an end.

An answering howl drew me through the trees. Moving on all fours, I came to the barrier that I sensed meant death to touch. Eyes watched me from the other side. Standing up, I stared into the golden depths of my mate as our minds melded. We shared a sense of wonder at the bond that linked us. Unlike my pitch black fur, his was almost silver. It matched the light that shone down upon us.

Gone were the complicated emotions that ruled our daily lives and deeper, simpler thoughts held sway. The loneliness that he'd felt for his entire life was gone now that we'd become bonded. *We will never be alone again,* he thought as he delved into my mind and saw the same loneliness inside.

Our bond will last until death, I replied. I didn't know how I knew this, but instinct told me that it was true.

We wanted to run beneath the moon together as we were meant to, but the barrier kept us apart. The transformation had left us both starving and we needed to hunt. Staring longingly at my mate, I turned away as I heard something in the distance. A sense of evil touched my mind and he felt it as well.

It's the soulless, he hissed. I instantly knew the creatures he was speaking of. They were dead humans that had been resurrected by foul magic. They were abhorrent to us and our first impulse was to hunt them down and rend them to pieces.

There are many, I noted as I picked up more and more of them. Our bond allowed us to share everything and he sensed them through me. We both knew that I was different from him, but we weren't sure why. I shouldn't have been able to feel the soulless in my head. My mate was worried that something was wrong with me, but we had to deal with the threat that was right here in front of us before we could focus on my strangeness.

We must kill them all, he said with grim purpose. Wordlessly, I agreed and loped off into the trees. I'd worry about whatever was wrong with me after we'd dealt with the undead.

Chapter Twenty-One

Now that I'd become a beast again, my senses were much stronger. I could see why my mate called the dead humans 'soulless'. They were empty shells that had been filled with unspeakable evil. Their master was somewhere close by, directing their attack. He was human, which meant he was beyond my ability to sense. Only my ears, nose and eyes would be able to detect him and he was staying at a safe distance.

Seeing one of the soulless ahead, I began to run on all fours. I quickly picked up speed and it sensed me moments before I closed in for the kill. Milky eyes turned to face me and it snarled, but my claws took its head off before it could react. Another one rose from the soil right in front of me. Curious as to what would happen, I grabbed it by the arm and tossed it at the fence. Bright sparks flew and the smell of cooking meat filled the air. The creature let out a buzzing scream of pain that hurt my head. Its agony only lasted for a moment before the fence killed it.

Joy in the hunt snared me as I went in search of more walking corpses to kill. Far in the distance, I heard another shifter let out an enraged yowl. It was a cat, a different species to me and hence my enemy. Another creature hissed and I heard bones being crushed by a powerful body. I was confused as to why there were other shifters in werewolf territory, but the soulless were my main concern right now.

I killed over a dozen of the corpses before their rudimentary intelligence allowed them to realize that I was too dangerous to approach. My mate had also hunted down his share of the vile things. The few remaining creatures melted into the ground before I could rend them apart. They burst out of the soil on the far side of the deadly barrier, safely out of my reach. As one, they turned and began to shamble away.

Faint with distance, my mate's panicked thought came to me. *They are going to attack the human! We have to save him!*

Still new to being a shifter, I could remember little of being human myself. My mate sent me a picture of a man. Average height and size, he was vaguely familiar. Although I immediately wanted to eat him, he was important to my mate somehow. For him, I'd try to rescue the human.

The barrier was too high to jump over, but I saw a way that I could scale it without coming to harm. A tree that was standing only a few yards away from the fence looked it might be large enough to hold my weight. My claws dug into the trunk and I climbed up to the top. I threw myself towards the barrier and let out a pained yelp when my foot brushed the top. My mate whined in sympathy. He'd felt my pain as if it were his own.

Landing on all fours, I limped off after the soulless. The pain was already fading and soon I was able to run at top speed again. Wind whipped my face as I galloped towards a building. My mate sent me the scent of the human that he wanted me to save. I smelled the man even before I reached the building. His scent was mixed with others that were also familiar. Two of the scents belonged to my mate and me. It was difficult to remember that we were usually human. I couldn't even remember any of the people we apparently lived with.

The entrance to the building had been destroyed by the soulless. I stepped over the door and entered a long, narrow passage. I didn't like being enclosed in the small space and ran to the end quickly. Another door was hanging open and I pushed it aside. The human that I'd been sent to save was surrounded by the walking dead. Fire spurted from the weapon in his hands and the soulless screamed in agony as they died. The man wasn't quite as helpless and feeble as I'd expected. He was afraid and his fear made him especially appealing. I began to salivate as my hunger rose.

Another door burst open and more of the vile beings swarmed inside. I let out a roar and the human turned. Terror sweat instantly poured from him. I had a brief image of him fleeing and of myself pursuing him. If he even twitched, I'd pounce. I'd crush his bones between my teeth and chew on his entrails.

The smell of decomposing flesh overwhelmed me, distracting me from my need to feed. Leaping into the room, I bounded past the stunned man and tore into the undead. I used my claws and teeth to tear them apart. Their rotting flesh and blood tasted horrible, but biting their heads and limbs off was the most effective way of dealing with them. Each one was nearly as strong as me, but they were slow and clumsy.

Before long, the soulless were also headless. They lay on the floor around me like leaves that had fallen from a tree. Rooted to the ground, the human watched with frightened eyes as I approached him. He was puny enough that I could have picked him up and snapped him in half. I kept the knowledge that this man was important to my mate firmly in my mind. Very carefully, I put my hand out. He flinched and his weapon shifted towards me minutely, but he didn't unleash the killing fire. I patted him on the head to indicate that I wasn't going to harm him. He made a sound of terror that very nearly made me drop to my knees and bite into the tender flesh of his stomach.

My upper lip lifted in a silent snarl as I fought the urge to bite the human's head off. My mate called to me through our link, sensing my inner battle. He wanted me to join him, but I had no way of entering the prison that held him. The human must have the means to rejoin me with my mate. Taking the weapon from him, I dropped it to the ground, then tucked him beneath my arm and ran back down the narrow passage.

Drawn to the one that I was linked to, I stopped at the door that kept us apart. He sent me a surge of approval when I placed the human carefully on the ground. *I kept him safe,* I said and sent him images of my battle with the soulless.

I wish I'd been with you, he replied wistfully. Hopefully, now that I'd brought him here, the human could open the door so my mate and I could hunt together. Now that the walking corpses were gone, we could concentrate on the many tasty animals there were to choose from in the forest.

Petrified, the human didn't realize what I wanted from him at first. I pointed at the door with my claws and gave him a light shove that almost sent him crashing into the deadly barrier.

Realizing what I wanted, he shook his head and said something that I didn't understand. I growled and took a threatening step towards him. He blanched and backed away, then went still when my mate made strange sounds with his mouth instead of speaking with his mind.

"Mark." It was a cross between a growl and a grunt. Linked to my other half, I understood that it was the human's name.

Astounded at being addressed by a being he saw as a mindless animal, Mark turned wondering eyes on my mate. "What the hell is happening here?" he asked plaintively. Through my bond, I actually understood his words this time.

I nudged Mark and he spun around to stare up at me. I pointed at the gate, urging him to open it. "You'll kill each other," he argued.

"No," my mate denied, but he couldn't articulate that we were bonded and that we'd never intentionally hurt each other. I lowered my head until I was eye to eye with the human and growled in warning.

Dazed, Mark took something out of his pocket and put his fingers on it. A few seconds later the barrier became safe. He put his hand on a device next to the door and the portal swung open. Fierce joy swelled inside me again as I bent to squeeze through the opening and joined my mate at last. Our yips of happiness became full throated howls of joy as we raced off into the trees.

Chapter Twenty-Two

When I woke, I was lying on my side with arms encasing me and a hard chest pressed up against my back. My mind was wide open and I knew that it was Reece holding me without needing to turn my head. I was naked, but at least I wasn't covered in blood this time. To my mortification, my companion was also unclothed.

Blinking at the weak early morning sunlight, I tried to remember how I'd ended up in Reece's enclosure. I was afraid to move because as soon as I did, he'd wake up. When he did, we'd both have to face this nightmare. His arms tightened and he pulled me against him more firmly. He nuzzled my neck in his sleep. My heartbeat increased at the brush of his lips on my skin and heat instantly flared. Sensing my panic, he woke, realized where we were and went still.

"Close your eyes!" I commanded.

"How did you get in here?" he asked in bewilderment.

I turned my head until we were staring at each other from a couple of inches away. The golden flecks in his eyes stood out more than usual, probably due to his recent change. "I don't know. All I know is that I'm naked and I want you to close your damn eyes."

A smile appeared before he could squelch it. "I've seen you naked before, Lexi," he pointed out but dutifully closed his eyes.

"I know," I muttered. "But that doesn't mean that I want you to see me naked again." He let go of me and I rolled free. Although I'd told him to close his eyes, I took a long look at him and hated the stab of desire that his chiseled body wrung from me.

"I can feel you staring at me," he said.

Irritated at being caught out, I stood and started walking towards the fence. "Just stay where you are until I find some clothes," I ordered.

"I left my backpack about thirty feet from the gate," he said helpfully. I knew he'd opened his eyes because I felt his desire rise. My face flamed crimson until I'd put enough trees between us to hide me from his view. I'd been told by several guys that I had a cute butt. Reece was the only one to have seen it in the flesh.

Long before I reached the fence, I smelled rotting meat. For a moment, I thought we must have fallen asleep near one of our meals. Then I spotted a pile of human bones and torn flesh. It wasn't until I saw a human head lying nearby that I realized it was a zombie. Its bones had been shattered and long, deep claw marks marred its flesh. One of us must have torn it apart while in wolf form.

Alarmed, I hurried on until I found the backpack. I passed more dismembered corpses along the way. Leaving the cargo pants for Reece, I pulled on the boxer shorts and his t-shirt. My clothes were in the enclosure next door, but they could wait for now. I needed to make sure the rest of the team was okay first.

Reece jogged out of the woods seconds after I'd dressed in his clothes. He'd been following right behind me and I hadn't even heard him. He ignored my embarrassment, equally disturbed at finding zombies in his enclosure. "We need to check on Mark," he said. I sensed his urgency, which spurred my own.

We could both sense that the electricity had been cut to the fence and I put my hand on the scanner to open the gate. Reece was right behind me when I pushed it open and started running. Kala and Flynn joined us when we were halfway back to the building.

Kala raised her eyebrows at what I was wearing. "That's an interesting choice of outfits. Did you forget to pack your bra?" I flushed, but I was too worried to get into a debate about my lack of underwear.

"Did you find any dead zombies in your enclosures?" Flynn asked.

"Yeah," I said. "It looked like we tore them apart."

"So, I wasn't just imagining it," Kala muttered. "This is bad." Her tawny hair was a mess and her eyes went wide with fear for our boss as we all picked up on the old scent of zombie rot. Some of them had gotten away from us and had made their way towards the base.

Flynn's expression was intent and he put on a burst of speed. "I hope Mark is okay."

We saw signs of a violent invasion when we reached the building. Scratches marred the walls. The door was shiny and new and had been replaced recently. Flynn was the first inside and we rushed down the hallway to the main area.

Kala wrinkled her nose before opening the door, which was also new. "I smell roasted zombie," she said and we all shared her fear at what we'd find on the other side.

Mark was sitting at the dining table, watching something on his tablet. He shot to his feet when we entered. He didn't seem to be hurt and we rushed to surround him to make sure.

I was surprised and hurt when he blanched and flinched away from me. "What's wrong?" I asked, wounded by his reaction.

He uttered a laugh that held no actual mirth, then seemed to take hold of himself. "What do you remember about the past three nights?"

Frowning, I thought back and, as per the last time, I remembered nothing. "Not much. I remember you escorting me to my gate, then nothing until I woke up this morning." I refrained from mentioning that I'd woken up in the enclosure next to mine.

Mark stared at me then switched his attention to Reece. "What do you remember?"

He shrugged uneasily. "The same as Lexi." He too avoided the secret that we shared.

Rubbing his face with both hands, Mark sank back into his seat. "I triggered both the indoor and outdoor cameras when I became aware that the compound was under attack. I've watched the footage a hundred times now and I still don't believe it."

"What happened?" Kala demanded and took the seat beside him. He allowed her to take his hand in hers. Obviously, she didn't make him as uncomfortable as I did. "We found zombie corpses in our enclosures and we can smell them in here, too."

There was no sign of the battle that must have raged inside the building. The Cleanup Crew had probably been called in to put the base to rights again.

"You might want to sit down for this," our boss warned us. We obeyed him and I had a horrible feeling in the pit of my stomach. Something strange had happened, and it had something to do with me. It was bad enough being turned into a werewolf, but I also had a weird and inexplicable connection to the undead.

"As you've probably guessed, the bokor sent his minions after us," Mark said. "I only realized that they were here when they broke down the doors. I had a flamethrower handy just in case this might happen, but there were too many of them to fight on my own."

"How are you still alive?" Reece asked. He'd taken the seat beside me and we were unconsciously leaning towards each other. I didn't want to admit it, but our bond seemed to be much stronger now. I was having a hard time keeping his thoughts separate from mine.

"Lexi saved me."

Dead silence ensued then it was broken by Kala's incredulous laugh. "How could she have saved you?" she asked. "She was locked in her enclosure just like the rest of us."

"I don't know how she did it, but she got out," Mark replied. He was watching me with a mixture of fear and wonder. "I'd just finished frying a pack of zombies when more of them broke in through the kitchen door. I heard a roar and a werewolf was standing in the doorway. I knew it had to be Lexi because it had black fur instead of silver and it was too small to be Reece."

I didn't particularly like being referred to as an 'it', but Reece put his hand on my arm before I could protest.

"Did she attack you?" Flynn asked. His tone was calm enough, but alarm showed in his hunched shoulders.

Mark shook his head. "No. She went for the zombies and ripped them to pieces." He went silent as he tried to gather the words to explain what I'd done next. "I thought she was going to kill me, but she walked over and patted me on the head."

"I did *what?*" My voice went so high that it was barely audible.

"I think you were trying to show me that you meant me no harm," he explained. "Then you tore my flamethrower out of my hands and carried me outside."

Flynn held his hand up to stop him. "She carried you how exactly?"

Mark mimed me tucking him under his arm. Kala sniggered and I came very close to giggling as well. I pictured a hulking, shaggy werewolf carrying a human like a football and Reece elbowed me in the side before I could descend into gales of hysterical laughter.

"I take it she took you to my enclosure," Reece said. It wasn't a question.

Nodding, Mark clenched his hands together. "She pointed at the door and pushed me towards it. She clearly wanted me to open it. I told her it would be dangerous." His voice trailed off and he shook his head in renewed bewilderment. "Then you said my name."

Reece's astonishment flooded into me. "I spoke?" At Mark's nod, he ran a hand through his short hair in confusion. "How is that even possible?"

"I have no idea," Mark replied. "You wanted me to open the door to your enclosure."

I had no recollection of these events and felt a creeping numbness trying to take over. Reece's arm brushed against mine, offering me moral support. He was just as dazed as I was. "I take it you let me in," I deduced.

"I said you'd kill each other, but you both indicated that you wouldn't," Mark said. "I opened the door and Lexi walked inside."

"Uh, oh," Kala said and I almost wished I could read her mind when a realization hit her.

"What?" I asked with extreme unwillingness.

"What if you two did the nasty while you were locked up together?"

"The nasty?" I asked, deliberately being obtuse about her question.

"Slept together," she clarified.

Reece and I shared a horrified look.

"Oh, my God," I breathed. "Would my birth control pills work when I'm a werewolf?"

We all turned to Mark, who had gone pale. His answer was far from reassuring. "I don't know."

Chapter Twenty-Three

To say I was inconsolable would be an understatement. I fled to my room in full hysterics. I was crying so hard that I could barely hear someone pounding on the door.

"Leave me alone!" I screamed loudly enough for whoever it was to get the hint. The rooms were soundproofed so we could sleep at night without every little noise waking us up, but our hearing was exceptional. We could detect it if someone knocked loudly enough.

I wasn't the only one who was panicked at the thought that I might be pregnant. Reece's worry leaked through the bond and so did his mental picture of me with a bellyful of babies. I was so shocked that my tears stopped and my mouth dropped open.

Leaping off the bed, I wrenched the door open and walked three doors down to the right. Reece's door was open a few inches and I knew he was inside.

Pushing the door open, I saw him sitting on the bed. Still shirtless, he'd changed into jeans that were almost threadbare in some places. He was leaning back against the pillows with one knee bent. His eyes were closed and he was listening to music through earphones. He seemed calm on the surface, but turmoil boiled inside him.

A pair of boots lay on the floor at the end of his bed. Snatching one up off the floor, I threw it at him as hard as I could. Sensing me, his eyes snapped open. He caught the projectile an instant before it would have hit him in the face.

Shutting off the music, he pulled the earphones off and regarded me warily. I knew my eyes were puffy and red and that I looked awful, but I was beyond caring about my appearance. "Am I going to have a litter?" It came out as a harsh croak.

His wariness changed to guilt when he realized I'd read what was on his mind. "I don't know, but I doubt it. I imagine there would be something written in the archives if mated werewolves tended to have litters."

I put my hands over my face and sank to my knees in despair. His feet thumped to the floor, then he swung me into his arms. Sitting on the edge of his bed, he pulled me onto his lap. "We don't know for sure that we even had sex," he said.

I shuddered and he held me more tightly. "You don't know that we didn't." My words were muffled by my hands.

My forehead was pressed against his chest and his chin was resting on the top of my head. It was almost peaceful being in his arms. It felt right, as if I belonged there and nowhere else. He sighed and I knew he felt it, too.

It hit me then, that this was the work of our hated bond. I struggled free of his arms and stood. "We can't let this happen again," I said in a low voice.

He knew I was talking about far more than me just sitting on his lap and he nodded wearily. "Mark will figure out how you got out of your enclosure. He'll make sure we're kept apart in the future."

"Good." My tone was wintry.

The shock of possibly being pregnant with multiple babies still hadn't worn off the next day. I couldn't face anyone in the team and spent the entire day in my room. Reading through the archives was a good way to keep my mind occupied. I carefully stayed away from any cases that were related to werewolves. Instead, I concentrated on reading up more about zombies.

It was almost a relief when someone knocked on my door later that night. I opened the door to see Kala on the other side. "The bokor is raising some more zombies," she said. "Are you up to taking a trip into the city?" Her gaze was assessing as she judged my mental state.

Bored with sitting inside my room, I nodded. I wasn't looking forward to being trapped in the SUV with the father of my hypothetical children, but it would only be for a short time. "I'll be right there," I said and she gave me a quick smile before darting off towards her own room.

I quickly packed a bag, then raced down the hallway to the stairs. The SUV was already running and we took off as soon as we were all inside.

Mark turned to speak to us. "The Zombie King may be more powerful than we first anticipated. I don't know how he tracked us to the compound, but he knows who we are and what we do. He'll be expecting us to try to stop him."

"What's he likely to do next?" Kala asked. "Will he come after us again, or will he target civilians?"

Mark shrugged. "It's difficult to predict the mind of a madman."

"Is he really insane?" Flynn asked.

"Power mad, maybe," Reece answered. "He's young, full of pride and smarting that we've either roasted, or torn his pets apart. He'll want revenge."

Mark nodded in agreement. "He's probably going to make a grand statement. I just don't know what it will be yet."

We closed in on the cemetery where the bokor had chosen to harvest his minions from this time. I sensed the awakening dead from two blocks away. "He's still there," I said. "I think he's raised a lot more thirty or forty zombies this time."

"How many more?" Flynn asked.

"Lots more," I replied dourly. I didn't have an exact number. I just knew that there were dozens of walking dead ready to do the sorcerer's bidding.

We parked close to the cemetery and Mark worked his electronic magic to kill the cameras. He always reset them before we left and before the cops turned up to investigate. We might not be so lucky this time. The bokor and his puppets were still here and I had a feeling they were waiting for us.

Mark motioned for us to gather around after we retrieved our flamethrowers from the back of the SUV. "I want you to hang back," he told me. "They can sense you once you get close and I don't want to tip them off that we're here until we're all in position."

It made sense and I nodded. To be honest, I wasn't thrilled with the thought of facing dozens of the creatures. Any reprieve would be welcome.

Once inside the gate, we split up to come at the mob from different angles. The usual eerie green fog held sway, limiting our visibility. Without the orderly rows of crypts and mausoleums to guide me, I'd have become lost.

A man was chanting in the midst of the graveyard. The language was unfamiliar and might have been Jamaican, but I couldn't be sure. All I knew was that the bokor was calling more minions forth and he seemed to be nearing the end of his ritual.

On that thought, a wash of power swept outwards. It blasted past me, making my ponytail stream out behind me. I sensed the undead forming in their graves and heard them trying to escape from their confinement. Only a few rows away from the center of the cemetery, I was frozen in fear as the zombies began to break free.

Kala screeched in fury and bright flames flared. That was the catalyst I needed to set me in motion. I flicked the safety off the flamethrower and pointed it at the closest corpse that was slowly shambling towards me. There was little sign of intelligence in its cloudy eyes. It was hungry and I was food. It sensed that I was a threat and hissed a warning to its brethren as more of them converged on me.

I set the reanimated corpse on fire and it squealed in agony, flailing its limbs uselessly. Once they caught, they burned quickly. Turning in a circle, I held the approaching creatures at bay with blasts of fire that shot out for ten feet around me. Elsewhere in the cemetery, the rest of the squad battled their share of minions.

I'd whittled the numbers down to a mere handful when a familiar face appeared. I only saw the bokor for a second before he raced off into the darkness. He was moving so fast that he didn't even notice me.

He wasn't alone. One of his minions was right on his heels. Unlike his master, the zombie sensed me and turned to stare as he ran past. Instead of the usual dull, milky gaze, this creature's eyes were clear. They were also filled with an evil cunning. His mind brushed mine and I sensed he was very different from the other shambling undead.

Completely naked, his flesh was still putrid, but he was held together better than most of his brethren. His face wasn't in such great shape. His nose was missing and half of his left cheek was gone, exposing his teeth and tongue. A few strands of long black hair clung to his scalp.

They were gone before I could react and someone called my name. Busy with torching zombies, I hadn't realized that the unknown watcher had returned. It was standing only a short distance away.

"Alexis," the figure said. The voice was female and her accent was foreign. How did she know my name? "Come to me, child," she urged. A shadowy shape appeared in the green fog and my feet started moving of their own volition. Whoever she was, she was using mind control, but it was different from the telepaths that we'd hunted down and destroyed. Instead of being overwhelming, it was almost seductive and impossible to resist.

Before I could move close enough to see the woman's face, a clammy hand fell on my shoulder. It spun me around until I was face to face with a reanimated corpse, breaking me from the spell. Another hand closed around my throat and I let out a pained shout as it tried to crush my windpipe.

I felt Reece approaching then the zombie was torn away and went flying through the air. Kala and Flynn arrived as well and all three unleashed their fire. Staggering out of the way, I leaned against Mark when he put his arm around my shoulder. Sirens wailed and I looked in the direction they were coming from. "The cops are coming," I rasped to Mark, knowing my hearing was far better than his.

There was no time to call the Cleanup Crew. We had no choice but to leave the charred remains of long dead corpses where they'd fallen. Mark reactivated the cameras once we were out of range and we piled into the SUV. One of the benefits of being a werewolf was rapid healing. My throat was already feeling much better and the bruises would fade within minutes.

We left the area as cop cars were converging on the now empty cemetery. The bloody circle where the bokor had performed his ritual was still there. I doubted that Mark would call in the Mind Sweepers to wipe anyone's memory since none of the corpses were actually moving. The police would probably think it was a horrible prank.

"I saw the Zombie King up close for a second," I said to the others when we were well on our way back to our base.

"What did he look like?" Flynn asked.

"He looked a lot like you," I said. "Except his eyes were brown rather than green. He couldn't be much older than us."

"Just as we thought. He's young and inexperienced," Mark said. He was watching me with concern. "How are you feeling?"

I wasn't sure if he was talking about me being strangled by a zombie, or the fact that I might be pregnant. "Numb," I replied. "Did any of you see the zombie that was with the bokor?"

"I thought we fried them all," Reece said, looking into the rearview mirror briefly.

"We missed one," I told him. "It was different from the others."

Mark's brow wrinkled. "Different how?"

"I think it was one of his early zombies and that it might have fed a few times. It seemed to be smarter than the others." It had been smart enough to run and avoid being burned to death.

Kala sighed unhappily. "That's just what we need, an intelligent zombie."

"I do not like the sounds of this," Flynn said. I couldn't help but share his concern. No one mentioned the woman that had been trying to lure me to her. I wasn't sure if she was real, or if I'd just imagined her. Fearing I was losing my mind, I stayed quiet. How could I explain the insidious power that she had over me to them when I didn't understand it myself?

Chapter Twenty-Four

It was difficult to fall asleep once I was tucked away in bed. My mind kept repeating the battle and I saw the exhilarated young bokor as he raced past me over and over. I also saw his undead shadow and the crafty evil in his eyes. When I did sleep, I dreamed of being watched.

Mark wanted to search the cemeteries again the next day, but he ordered me to remain behind when he saw how tired I was. I was grateful for a chance to be alone for a few hours. The team knew the signs to look for in the graveyards and we all had the bokor's scent now. Any of us could follow his trail if we came across it again.

I didn't want to be cooped up in my room, so chose to sit on the couch to study the archives. It was strangely lonely being by myself, which was unusual. I was used to being on my own and had never had a problem with solitude before. While I was eating lunch, I realized the real reason for my uneasiness. Reece was too far away for me to be able to pick up his thoughts clearly. Sometime during the past few weeks, I'd become used to having him in my mind. I could still sense him, but it was distant.

After my short lunch break, I continued to dig through the PIA files. I read through all of the records on zombies and none of them shed much light on our current situation. There were thousands of other records and I wanted to read them all. It would take me a very long time to do so, but I was now a permanent member of the squad and I had plenty of time to kill.

Niggling curiosity had me sorting the files into their various categories. Mark knew a lot about shifters and it made sense that he'd learned what he knew from the files. It was time for me to learn more about my species. I started reading through the earliest records of werewolves and other shifters.

There was a lot of speculation about how shifters had come to be. Some thought it was a curse. Others thought it had something to do with the old Norse gods. One theory was that a deal had been made with the devil. No one knew for sure how we and other monsters had been created. We'd always been around and there had always been brave or foolhardy humans to fight us.

Scrolling through the files, I came across a record that was much more modern. It had been recorded only a couple of years before my birth. Opening it, I saw a picture of Mark with a woman and a small child. He was young, in his early twenties and he looked happy. In the next photo, his wife and daughter were in pieces. They'd been torn apart by something that had big teeth and long claws.

A chill seeped into my bones as I read about Mark's introduction into the dark underworld that few humans knew about. He'd hunted down the rogue shifter that had murdered his family. He'd gotten his justice and in doing so, he'd come to the attention of the PIA. Instead of wiping his memory, they'd approached him and had offered him a job. He'd become a federal agent and had been fighting creatures like me ever since.

Setting my laptop aside, I brought my knees up to my chest and wrapped my arms around them. What kind of man would save and then raise three shifters? We were the same type of monsters that had killed and eaten his wife and daughter. He should hate and fear us, but he felt genuine affection for the whole squad, including me.

Most agents would have set me on fire when I'd burst into the base in werewolf form. I didn't remember it, but he must have been petrified. He hadn't allowed me to watch the footage because he didn't want me to see myself when I was an animal. I only had my imagination to go on. He was a very brave man and we were lucky to have him as our boss.

Needing a break, I shut down my laptop, then picked up the remote control with the intention of turning on the TV. My cell phone rang before I could activate the television. It was Mark. "What's wrong?" I asked as soon as I answered the phone. I had a feeling he wasn't calling just to check up on me.

"Agent Garrett is on his way to pick you up," Mark replied. "The voodoo priestess that we questioned on our first day in New Orleans just tracked us down. She had some interesting information." His tone led me to believe it was more frightening than interesting. "Reece should be there in a few minutes and he can fill you in. Bring your rifle," he ordered before hanging up.

Slipping my phone back into my pocket, I leaped off the couch and dashed upstairs. My sniper rifle was in the backpack inside my closet. I snagged the pack and dumped it on the bed, then rapidly changed my clothes. Dressed in a black t-shirt and khaki cargo pants, I strapped my holster on, then covered it with my lightweight military style jacket. Black boots finished off my outfit. Snatching up the tablet from my bedside table, I tucked it beneath my arm and raced downstairs.

I left via the door in the kitchen that led to the front of the compound just as the SUV arrived. I climbed into the passenger seat even before the car had come to a complete stop. Reece's scent surrounded me when I pulled the door shut. He used a pine scented soap that I found very appealing. "What's the situation?" I asked crisply as he set the vehicle in motion.

He smiled wryly at my formal tone, knowing I wanted to keep the conversation focused on work rather than on our personal problems. "The priestess tracked us down when we were a few blocks away from her store. She said that the bokor reanimated the wrong corpse and that New Orleans is now in far more peril than before."

"I knew there was something off about that zombie," I said almost beneath my breath. He heard me, of course.

"Apparently, the zombie you saw with the bokor was a powerful necromancer when he was alive. He terrorized the city when he was at the height of his power over a hundred and fifty years ago."

"This is bad." I gave myself mental points for being a master of the understatement.

"It won't be long before the Zombie King loses control of the necromancer," he said. "He's not going to be any match for him when he regains his intelligence."

"What's going to happen when the necromancer takes over?"

"He'll most likely start raising other zombies and set them on the civilians. They'll need to feed to increase their strength."

"What's our plan?"

"Mark wants to stay close to the action. We're going to patrol the cemeteries until we see signs of activity. When we do, we'll move in and try to stop them before they can raise more corpses."

"Does Mark still have access to the CCTV cameras?"

"He does and we'll all have to monitor our tablets." It would be a fairly boring job watching the monitor nonstop. It would be easy to allow my eyes to glaze over and to miss something important. Picking up on that thought, Reece addressed my concern. "He's hoping your inbuilt zombie radar will aid us."

We hadn't really talked about why I could sense the walking dead, and I wasn't comfortable bringing it up now, so I simply nodded in agreement.

It was only late afternoon now and nightfall was still hours away. We drove into the heart of the city and parked out front of a quaint café. The team was huddled inside around two small round tables. Kala smiled and motioned for me to take the seat beside hers. "I ordered you a coffee," she said and pointed to a large mug when I sat down.

Picking up the mug, I took a swallow. It was hot, strong and perfect. "Thanks," I said and nudged her arm with mine. I'd never had a sister or a best friend before and she was shaping up to be a cross between the two. It would be nice to have a female to talk to and to confide in. That had been lacking in my life pretty well forever. Losing my mother when I'd been a baby meant I had trouble connecting to other females. I wasn't sure why Kala and I got along so well when we were technically species that tended to dislike each other.

Flynn held his tablet in his hands, watching the screen intently. It would take time for the bokor to set up his ritual. He'd have to wait until the cemetery of his choice emptied out before he could begin. Mark had tweaked the tablets so we each had three areas to monitor rather than just two this time. The café had been a strategic choice. It was in the heart of New Orleans and it would take us mere minutes to reach even the most distant cemetery.

I'd almost finished my coffee when two plain clothes cops entered the café. They hesitated for a moment before heading straight to our table. I recognized them as being the same two officers who'd been investigating the zombie break-ins. The older man was about Mark's age and had weary, jaded brown eyes that assessed us quickly but thoroughly.

The other officer was in his early twenties and seemed new to the job. He was average in height, stocky in build and had short blond hair. His eyes were light blue and inquisitive. He studied our faces intently. His gaze lingered on me for longer than could be considered polite by most standards. I wasn't used to being stared at with such blatant hunger. Reece tensed and his jealousy flared. Mark sent him a warning look as if he could hear the low growl that had started up in Reece's throat. It was so quiet that even I could barely hear it.

"Calm down, Rex," Kala breathed. The hated nickname broke through his instinct to defend what he thought of as his. I felt his possessiveness and was fuming by the time the two cops came to a stop beside our tables.

"Can I see some ID?" the older cop asked.

Mark fished inside his jacket and produced his PIA identification. "Is there a problem, officers?"

The older cop examined the ID, wrinkling his brow at the acronym that he hadn't heard of before. He didn't want to broadcast his lack of knowledge and handed back the wallet. "What do you folks know about the graveyard desecrations that have occurred in our city lately? Particularly, the one that occurred last night?"

"Very little, I'm afraid," Mark replied as he tucked his ID away. "I'm sure you know more than we do."

"Do you know anything about the CCTV cameras being tampered with?" the younger cop asked. His tone was mild, but his body language was aggressive. His jaw was thrust forward and he leaned over the table threateningly.

Reece slouched back in his chair and eyed the cop lazily. "We're federal agents, not computer hackers," he lied with a touch of contempt.

The older cop pointed at me without looking directly at me. "I highly doubt that this young lady is a federal agent. In fact, I doubt she's even old enough to legally be away from her parents."

"I'm eighteen," I said in self-defense.

That brought a smile to the younger cop's face. "Are you now?" he asked. His eyes dropped from my face down to my chest and lingered. My breasts weren't exactly impressive, but they captured his attention anyway.

Reece started growling again, which made my temper flare. I was within an inch of snapping at him to calm down when Mark spoke. "In the spirit of co-operation, is there anything you can tell us about the desecrations?"

The younger cop's eyes left me reluctantly as his partner answered. "A man has been spotted lurking around the cemeteries at night. He's in his early twenties, has dark skin and is most likely in a cult." Digging in his jacket, he pulled out a plastic evidence bag with the bokor's calling card inside. "We have video footage of him and some accomplices messing around in the cemeteries and breaking into a jewelry store. His accomplices were strong enough to pull the back door completely off its hinges. The footage is grainy, but we're pretty sure they were high on something. The perp is apparently calling himself the Zombie King," he said with a wry smile.

"He's probably breaking into graves and setting the bodies on fire as some kind of initiation ritual," the younger cop said. "This sort of thing happens all the time in New Orleans. There's really no need for the feds to be here. We can handle this ourselves."

Neither man had offered their identification and Mark didn't ask for it. We weren't interested in working with the local cops. They'd just be a hindrance to our investigation. Especially since neither of them questioned why such ancient bodies contained flesh rather than just being bones. The fire had burned up the corpses pretty well, but it hadn't melted the flesh entirely. Surely whoever examined the bodies would figure that out and would inform the police.

"You're probably right," Mark said after examining the card and handing it back. "But we're going to hang around for a couple more days, just in case."

Not particularly happy with that reply, the cops didn't linger. The blond sent a smirk at me over his shoulder before he stepped outside.

Reece's hands were clenched on the table and his body was almost vibrating with anger.

"You're not going to unzip your pants and mark your territory are you?" Kala asked, then sniggered.

"Keep yourselves under control," Agent Steel said in a calm tone. "The last thing we need is to make the local cops suspicious of us."

Reece had done it for me a few times, so I tried sending him soothing thoughts. His gaze snapped to me in astonishment, but his fists unclenched and his shoulders relaxed. I was as surprised as him that it worked and that his tension eased.

With the crisis over, Mark gestured to the tablets that were sitting face down on the table. "We need to stay sharp and remain focused. The priestess warned us that the bokor can raise a lot more zombies now that he has a pet necromancer on hand."

"How many more?" I asked uneasily.

"Possibly an entire cemetery with one single ritual," was his bland, yet highly disturbing reply.

Chapter Twenty-Five

With visions of a zombie apocalypse running through my mind, I did my best to focus on the cemeteries on my monitor. The images were small, but not so tiny that we wouldn't be able to see anyone entering the premises.

As darkness began to close in, we piled into the SUV. We drove through the streets slowly, cruising past the cemeteries closely enough for me to be able to sense any undead activity if it were to arise. Mark monitored both his and Reece's tablets.

Shortly after true night fell, I felt the unseen eyes of the mystery woman watching me. No matter where we went, she always seemed to be there. Reece sent frequent glances at me in the rearview mirror. He could sense my fear, but probably thought it was to do with the bokor and his undead slaves.

I felt the swell of power when we were about to make our third trip past one of the larger graveyards. "Stop!" I said and the SUV lurched to a halt. One look at my white face told everyone that we'd hit the jackpot.

"I want you to try to take the bokor down from a distance," Mark said to me as we parked on a quiet side street.

My mind was chaotic, but my hands knew what to do. They assembled my sniper rifle as they had done thousands of times before. I could move a lot faster now and I had the rifle ready in less than thirty seconds. I slung it over my shoulder as I climbed out of the SUV. My team mates moved in to surround me. They shielded me from the few pedestrians who were still out and about. Seeing someone openly carrying a sniper rifle would result in an instant panic.

Mark didn't switch off the cameras this time now that the cops were on to that trick. Instead, we entered the cemetery through a small, all but forgotten side gate that didn't have a camera watching it.

The green fog had spread more rapidly and far more widely than usual. It licked at the very edges of the grounds and spilled over onto the sidewalk. The murk was going to make scoping out the target a lot harder. Armed with flamethrowers, the team remained with me as we closed in on the center of the boneyard.

I heard chanting and my heart started hammering faster. The ritual was well underway. If I didn't stop the Zombie King, he was going to raise a far larger army of walking corpses this time.

Using a crypt to brace my rifle on, I peered through my scope. At first, the green fog obscured my vision. All I saw was the shadowy outlines of more crypts and mausoleums. Then a figure stepped into view.

My target's expression was close to ecstasy as he walked in a circle. He held a bowl in one hand and the other dipped inside to wet his fingers, then splatter the red liquid on the ground. His reanimated right hand man followed him. Shuffling a few steps behind, the zombie stared at his master avidly.

The bokor's voice rose and I had the feeling his ritual was almost done. I sighted on his chest, but before I could pull the trigger, the zombie struck. He punched his fist through his master's back, cutting off his words. Pulling his hand free, he licked the blood that coated his rotting flesh.

Staggering sideways, the Zombie King tried to run. His feet tangled and he fell, but his minion caught him before he hit the ground. Shoving his hand into the hole he'd already made in the human's back, he fished around until he found the object he wanted and ripped it loose. He held the heart of his former master up and studied it as if it were a glass of fine wine. Then he stuffed the bloody morsel into his mouth.

Chewing and then swallowing the heart, he wasn't finished desecrating the now deceased Zombie King's body. He wrenched his former master's head from side to side, then pulled it clean off his shoulders. Standing, the necromancer brought the head down on the corner of a crypt. Blood and brains oozed out as the head split open.

I made an involuntary sound of revulsion and the necromancer looked straight at me. Now that he was aware of me, he could sense my thoughts and instantly knew that I was dangerous. I picked up his unease that he'd never encountered anything like me before.

Instead of eating the brains that were sluggishly sliding down his arms, he flicked them at the ground and walked in a rapid circle. I couldn't understand the words that he was chanting, but I knew what he was doing. He was trying to complete the ritual. If he did, we would shortly be surrounded by his undead kin.

He opened his mouth to shout a final command and jerked back when my bullet slammed into his chest. Hissing in rage, his malignant gaze pierced the fog and latched onto me again. He wanted me dead with a rage that made me blanch.

"Aim for its head," Kala reminded me.

I readjusted my aim, but I was too late. The necromancer finished walking the circle and splashed the fluids of his dead master onto the ground. I could smell blood all around us and guessed that most of the graves had been marked. The necromancer shouted something, but my second bullet disintegrated his jaw so the words came out mangled.

With a malevolent glare over his shoulder, he turned and shambled into the shadows. He was now missing his lower jaw as well as his cheek and nose. With luck, he wouldn't be able to perform another ritual now that he couldn't speak.

While I'd hindered his spell, it hadn't been enough to halt it completely. Creaking and groaning, crypts and mausoleums began to spill open. My early intervention meant that only the graves at the center of the cemetery were affected. Instead of hundreds of foes to face, there were merely dozens.

Sensing us, the newly risen turned to attack. Far more power had been used to raise these corpses and they were almost fresh. Their flesh was only semi rotted and only the slight smell of rancid meat gave them away. All were naked, their clothing having long since disintegrated. The necromancer was good, but not even he could conjure up clothing out of thin air.

Moaning and gibbering with unholy hunger, they lurched towards us. I shouldered my rifle and took the flamethrower that Flynn handed to me. Orange flames flared and we formed a circle against our opponents.

Shrieks of pain and rage rang out as we lit up the night. The undead were slow to catch on, but they eventually realized that trying to eat us was very bad for their health. Twenty or so broke off from the main attack and went in search of less deadly food.

"Spread out and go after them," Mark ordered.

Fear held me in its sweaty grip, but I forced my feet into motion and followed a trio of shambling creatures. The instinct to run was strong, but I had a job to do and I wasn't going to let the team down again. If I'd been faster to pull the trigger, I could have stopped this from happening.

Unlike me, Reece felt no fear at all. He was finding joy in the hunt, as were Kala and Flynn. If I hadn't been so creeped out by the zombies, I'd be feeling a lot happier about going after our prey.

With the final zombie in ashes, I lowered my flamethrower and realized that I was all alone. The others were spread throughout the cemetery, still chasing their targets. Feeling the strange female's eyes on me, I tried to flee. She caught me in her spell before I could take more than two steps.

"Alexis," the musical, accented voice said, stopping me in my tracks. "Come to me."

Unwillingly, I turned around and saw her through the fog. She was just an indistinct outline. All I could make out was long, dark hair and skin that was so pale that it almost seemed to glow in the dark. I struggled against the grip that she had on me, but I lurched towards her anyway. In the back of my mind, I felt Reece's alarm.

"Come to me," she crooned and I was helpless to disobey her.

I was only thirty feet away from her when a hand came down on my shoulder. Reece spun me around. Concern poured off him in waves. Seeing my dazed expression, his brow furrowed. "What's wrong?"

Sending a look back over my shoulder, the area was empty and I could no longer sense the strange female. "Nothing," I lied. How could I possibly explain the shadowy figure to him when he hadn't even seen her?

"Didn't you hear me calling you?"

"No." I hadn't heard anything but the dark figure commanding me to go to her.

Mark reached us before he could question me further. "Did we get them all?" he asked me.

Snapping out of my daze, I turned in a full circle and didn't feel any more undead creatures. "I think so. Did you get the necromancer?"

Agent Steel shook his head reluctantly. "I didn't see any sign of him. I think he fled while we were taking care of his minions."

I didn't find it amusing at all that the minion had become the master and now had servants of his own. I was too horrified at seeing him tear his master's head off and crack it open like an egg. The image almost made my stomach heave and Reece put his hand on my back, sensing my queasiness. He was frustrated that he didn't know what was going on with me. I was already weird by their standards and I didn't want to ostracize myself even further by admitting that a strange female was stalking me.

We couldn't hear any police sirens yet, so Mark called the Cleanup Crew while the rest of us went about setting lids back on crypts. We tossed the bodies randomly inside the graves so the Crew wouldn't have to dispose of quite as many corpses. They'd clean up the rest of the mess and no one would know what had happened this night.

Unfortunately, the undead necromancer was still out there and this wasn't over yet. Our initial target was now dead, but only part of our mission had been accomplished. He'd unleashed a far greater danger that we'd have to take care of before our job would be done.

Headless and abandoned, the body of the bokor lay face down on the ground. His cracked open skull lay a few feet away. The Zombie King had proven to be no match for the servant that he'd raised. Did that make the necromancer a Zombie Emperor? Our new foe would be far more of a challenge for us. He could cause untold destruction before we finally took him down. I felt weary just thinking about chasing after him and attempting to stop him before he could raise an army.

We were subdued as we drove back to the compound. Kala and Flynn sat closer to me than usual so our knees and shoulders were touching. It was comforting to know I wasn't the only one who was uneasy.

It had been difficult enough to try to predict what the Zombie King would do. Now we had to anticipate the moves of a necromancer that had died over a hundred and fifty years ago. Flynn was good at anticipating what human monsters might do, but even he might not be up to the task of figuring out what our undead foe had planned.

Chapter Twenty-Six

We had a late dinner and I ate only half of my meal before pushing my plate away. I took a long shower, but I couldn't banish the thoughts and images that kept swirling around inside my head. I saw the Zombie King's skull crack open again and again and knew I'd never get to sleep with that image in my mind.

Three doors down from me, Reece was just as restless. He was picking up on my emotions and I wondered just how much of what I was thinking was getting through to him. Lying down, I forced my mind to be calm and did my best to mask my emotions from him. He did the same and I finally managed to fall asleep.

I'd forgotten to switch the alarm on and slept for longer than usual. When I woke, everyone had already started their daily routine. Too tired and cranky to train, I ate breakfast, then climbed back up the stairs. Mark stood at the computer table, reading a report on one of the screens. Seeing me out of the corner of his eye, he pressed a button on the table and the screen went blank. Whatever he'd been reading was probably above my clearance level.

"How are you feeling?" he asked.

"I'm okay. It was a shock to see the necromancer kill his master." I'd been the only one to witness the sudden betrayal. The others had seen the beheaded corpse, but they'd been spared seeing his head being cracked open and his brains being scooped out. "I'm sorry I couldn't stop the ritual in time," I said in a small voice.

Mark touched my arm. "This isn't your fault, Lexi. It's thanks to your quick action and skill that we only had a few zombies to kill rather than an entire cemetery full of them."

Looking into his eyes, I saw no hint of fear or revulsion towards me. He was totally comfortable being around us, except for when I'd saved him from the zombies while I was a werewolf. "I read the file about what happened to your family," I blurted, but kept my voice quiet enough so that the others didn't overhear me.

He lowered his voice as well. "I wondered how long it would take you to find it."

He wasn't angry that I'd pried into his life. In fact, he gave me the impression that he'd expected me to. "How can you stand to be around us?" I asked. I was anguished for him, unable to imagine how horrible it would have been to lose his wife and child so violently.

"Shape shifters aren't inherently evil," he said. "Most of you avoid killing humans."

"Was the attack on your family just random bad luck then?"

He stared past me, eyes unfocused. "No. It was very deliberate. The file doesn't mention what I used to do for a living," he said softly. "I worked for the CIA and I was close to cracking a major case regarding the disappearance of dozens of people over a ten year period."

"A shape shifter was behind the disappearances?" I hazarded a guess.

"He was a local firefighter and even helped to search for the victims. He had us all fooled," Mark said with a hint of derisiveness that was aimed at himself. "Then I found a clue that led me straight to him. He knew I was closing in and he tried to distract me by killing my wife and daughter." His grief was still there after twenty years and I saw the pain in his eyes. "It looked like an animal had torn them apart, but I knew he had something to do with it."

"What did you do?"

"I hunted him down and confronted him. He admitted that he'd killed the missing people and described what he'd done to my wife and daughter in detail." He grimaced and his gaze went distant. "Looking back now, I could see that he was trying to goad me into attacking him mindlessly. The full moon was still days away and he couldn't change into a werewolf. He was more vulnerable in human form." His gaze returned to the here and now. "I kept my calm and he came at me. I put a bullet in his shoulder. I guessed that he wasn't human when the bullet was expelled and his flesh healed." His smile was wry. "My next bullet went into his brain."

"Did that kill him?"

"No, but half a dozen more did the trick."

"That's good to know." We might be strong, but we were far from indestructible.

"You want to know how I can bring myself to be around shifters after one murdered my family." It wasn't a question, but I nodded anyway. "I was approached by the PIA after they discovered that I knew about supernatural creatures. I learned everything I could about your kind after I joined the agency. Shifters are only evil in their animal forms if they're evil as humans," he explained. "The werewolf that killed my family was a sadist. He was also an alpha, which gave him more power than normal shifters. I now believe that he was able to retain his human intelligence when he shifted. That's how he was able to target my family."

According to him, Reece and I were able to think and communicate while we were transformed. I guessed it was possible for another shifter to do so as well. "I still don't get why you chose to take the squad under your protection."

"They were little more than babies when they were captured," he said simply. "They weren't given a choice about becoming shifters. They were injected with the virus and I knew it would take years before it would transform them. They'd been stolen from their families, all of whom were probably killed by the rival organization. I believed I could raise them to be caring and compassionate human beings."

"You hoped that if you brought them up properly, they wouldn't turn into evil monsters," I concluded.

"Exactly."

We shared a smile, then something he said came back to me. "How did you know the shifter was an alpha?"

He looked down at the floor then up at me again. "At the next full moon, his pack hunted me down and tried to take their revenge on me."

"He had a pack?" I knew wolves were pack animals, but I didn't know that werewolves were as well. I always imagined they were solitary creatures who hunted alone. I should have known better after he'd told me that I'd demanded to be let into Reece's cage. That reminded me of my possible pregnancy, which was something I was desperately trying to avoid thinking about at all.

"He had a mate and four pack members." Mark winced at the memory. "They had my scent and tracked me to my home. The alpha female almost killed me." He pulled his shirt out of his pants and lifted it to show me long faded claw marks on his stomach.

"Ouch!" I grimaced in sympathy.

"I'd loaded my gun with silver bullets after I'd learned that werewolves were real. You don't need a kill shot to cause severe damage."

"Did you kill them all?"

"No," he shook his head. "I took two of them down, but the alpha female and two remaining pack members ran off. I tracked them back to their den, but they were gone." His expression was haunted and I dropped the subject before I could cause him more pain.

Now that I'd been reminded of my status as a potential mother, I couldn't get the idea out of my head. It was too soon to take a pregnancy test. I was pretty sure I'd have to wait for a couple of weeks before anything would show. Entering my room, I put my hand on my stomach and imagined it swollen and distended with multiple babies.

Some girls grew up wanting to be moms, but I'd never been one of them. Children were years away for me, if I had any at all. I'd been planning on joining the army and had intended to serve for as long as they'd wanted me. That dream was dead now. It had been torn away from me on the night that Lust had bamboozled Reece into having sex with me.

Lying down on my bed, I stared up at the ceiling and brooded about my uncertain future.

Chapter Twenty-Seven

Kala knocked on my door to fetch me for lunch, waking me from a light doze. I felt bad for slacking off, so agreed to train with her when we were finished eating. Not only was she faster, stronger and far more skilled than me, she also outweighed me. She pinned me down for the fifth time in a row and I was thoroughly sick of being beaten by then.

"Getting angry won't help," she said, easily holding me down with her knees on my shoulders. I took a swipe at her, but she saw it coming and leaned back before my fist could connect with her chin. "Nice try," she grinned.

Annoyed almost beyond reason, I looked her dead in the eye. Reece had taught me to control my anger, but it was about to spill out again. I didn't want to hurt her, I just wanted to move her. "Get off me," I ordered in the same tone that my father used the few times that I'd been stupid enough to push him to the edge.

She reacted instantly. Letting go of my shoulders, she rolled off me and crouched on the floor, cringing away as if expecting a blow. Realizing what she'd done, her mouth dropped open. Reece and Flynn were sparring in the boxing ring. Both stopped to stare at me.

"What?" I asked, climbing to my feet and brushing my clothes off.

"Kala just obeyed you as if you were her alpha," Flynn said in astonishment.

"Cats have alphas?" I asked in surprise.

"All shifters have alphas, even if they refer to them as something else," Reece replied. "There's always either an alpha male or female whenever there is a pack. They sometimes have both, if they're mated."

"But we're not a pack," I said, thoroughly confused as to why my command had worked.

"Aren't you?" Mark asked. He'd been sitting at the dining table, but had approached when he'd sensed trouble brewing.

"We're not even from the same species," I pointed out.

Kala was just as disturbed as I was about her reaction. "Maybe we don't have to be the same species to think of each other as pack." In her place, it would be a pride rather than a pack, but it was the same concept. I had no idea what Flynn's kin would be called. As far as I knew, snakes didn't run together in groups.

"You know what this means," Flynn said. A smile was trying to appear, but he kept it under control and spoke solemnly. "You two really are an alpha couple," he said when no one else spoke.

It was fairly obvious that Reece was an alpha. He tended to take charge whenever Mark let him. While Mark was our boss, Reece was the real leader of the squad.

"If Lexi really is an alpha, then she'll be able to ignore your direct order," Kala said to Reece. Her golden brown eyes were excited by the idea. Like me, she wasn't fond of being told what to do. She'd get a kick out of it if I could remain independent of Reece's superior power.

Reece had been the one to turn me and we were living in the same building. I guessed that meant we were a pack. It had never occurred to me that I should think of him as my alpha. Maybe because I was apparently one myself. The thought that I might be his equal instead of his subordinate didn't displease me at all.

Contemplating the notion, Reece's curiosity had him dropping his gloves and climbing out of the ring. Sweat dripped down his torso and it was all I could do not to follow the trail of moisture down to his abs. I almost backed up a step at his intent stare. Only pride made me stay in place.

Standing over me, he looked into my eyes. "Make me a cup of coffee," he ordered.

His tone was imperious and my hackles immediately rose. "Make it yourself!" I said in outrage. "I'm not your servant!"

Kala sniggered and Flynn choked on a laugh. Reece raised an eyebrow in sardonic amusement then looked into my eyes again. His became melting golden pools that I wanted to drown in. "Please?" he entreated.

His tone was seductive and something clenched in my stomach. My mind went hazy and when it cleared, I was halfway to the kitchen. Whirling around, I pointed my finger at him accusingly. "Don't try your Jedi mind tricks on me, Agent Garrett!"

Flynn slapped his thigh and laughed. "You almost had her," he chortled.

Kala was laughing as well. She seemed to have forgiven me for ordering her around. I was still new to being both a shifter and a member of their squad. It was going to take time for me to fit in and to find my place.

We showered, changed and headed back to New Orleans well before dark. The same two police officers who had questioned us showed up while we were cruising the streets. They watched our SUV suspiciously and followed us at a distance.

"I don't think we're going to be able to shake them, boss," Reece said after keeping track of them in the rearview mirror for several blocks.

"I'm hungry," Kala complained, unconcerned that we had a tail.

I was hungry, too. My stomach had been rumbling for the past hour, making Flynn grin every time it sounded. Being a wereconstrictor, he didn't get quite as ravenous as the rest of us, but even he had to eat regularly.

"We'll stop at the next restaurant we see," Mark said. "The officers will probably question us again and I want everyone to stay in control of their tempers." His warning was directed at Reece.

"I'll control myself if they keep their eyes to themselves," he replied moodily. I knew his feelings of ownership and protectiveness stemmed from our bond, but I still wasn't a fan of his overbearing attitude.

Kala smothered a grin with her hand when I rolled my eyes dramatically. "Alphas," I complained in a whisper.

"You should know," she whispered back. "You have quite the temper yourself." She winked to show she had no hard feelings about my ability to boss her around. I suspected it was a once off that wouldn't happen again anytime soon. She wasn't exactly meek herself and she was strong enough to resist orders from a wolf.

We found a large restaurant that was half filled with patrons. We drew curious stares when we entered and were seated at a table for six. I ended up sitting across from Reece, with my back to the door. I trusted the team to make sure no one attacked me. Still, I glanced backwards every now and then anyway. Flynn was sitting to my right and he was just as unhappy with our seating arrangement. Knowing the cops were following us had us all jumpy. We were the good guys and we were being stalked as if we were responsible for the desecrations and robberies.

Reece's shoulders went stiff when the two plain clothes cops entered. Sitting beside him, Kala's upper lip lifted in a silent snarl. Mark sat at the head of the table as usual. His pointed glance had them both relaxing again. We'd just finished ordering and the waitress had brought our drinks. I closed my hands around my mug of coffee to keep them occupied. I tended to fidget when I was nervous and these two cops made me very fidgety. Especially the younger one.

Two sets of footsteps approached and I felt one of the men right behind me. I refused to turn around and acknowledge them. The young blond cop stood close enough for me to feel the warmth of his body against my back. Reece stared at him coldly until he backed away a step.

"Fancy seeing you all here," the older cop said in a falsely jovial tone. "Officer Mallory and I were hoping we'd run into you again."

"We've just ordered dinner. You're welcome to join us," Mark said politely.

"We can't stay," Mallory replied. I didn't like him being so close and my whole body was tense. I wasn't sure what I'd do if he touched me even accidentally. Either punch him in the face, or pull my gun and blast a few holes in him. Neither impulse would be a good idea. "We just wanted to ask if you've made any progress in your case," he added.

"Not yet," Agent Steel replied. His posture was far more relaxed than mine or Reece's. Kala chewed on a breadstick and eyed the two cops almost insolently. Flynn had half turned to keep them in his line of sight.

"You'll let us know as soon as you learn anything?" the older cop said. It was a mystery how they knew we were here in relation to the desecrations. Instinct maybe. Either that or nothing else of interest was happening in the city.

"Of course," Mark replied.

I cringed when I felt Mallory lean in close. "I'll see you again soon," he whispered in my ear.

Kala and Mark automatically reached for Reece when he tensed. Flynn's hand was on my wrist, keeping me in my seat. I'd swiveled around to watch the cops leave and was startled to realize I was growling low in my throat.

"Down, girl," Flynn said quietly.

Kala giggled and the tension broke. We'd been feeding off each other's anger. I hadn't felt physically threatened by Mallory, but I didn't like him being behind me. His intentions were fairly obvious. He wanted to get me naked. He couldn't have been clearer about that if he'd shouted it to the entire room.

"I thought you were going to tear his throat out," Kala said.

"So did I for a second there," I agreed. If Flynn hadn't restrained me, the cop would probably be lying on the floor spurting blood right now.

"I'm glad you all managed to contain your anger," Mark said dryly.

I flushed in embarrassment and dropped my eyes. "Sorry," I mumbled.

"You're young," he said, meaning both my actual age and my status as a werewolf. "You'll learn control eventually." He switched his attention to Reece. "You, however, should know better and you have no excuse."

Reece flushed as well, but he didn't look away. "It's the bond," he explained. "It won't allow me to tolerate someone poaching on my territory."

Kala turned laughing eyes on me. "Did you hear that, Alexis? You belong to Garrett now."

My embarrassment instantly tripled and I pushed away from the table. "I'm going to the ladies room," I announced. I needed to distance myself from everyone, even if it was just for a few minutes.

I took my time in the bathroom then washed my hands and leaned over the sink to splash water on my face.

"You've grown into a beautiful woman, Alexis," a voice said and the light went out.

My gaze darted to the mirror, but no one was there. I whirled around and a woman was standing only inches away from me. We were about the same height, but her face was hidden in a shadow that was so deep that my eyes couldn't penetrate it. I sensed that the shadow wasn't real and that she was clouding my mind.

"How do you know me?" I asked. Up this close, she emanated a sense of unnaturalness that had my hackles rising again. Her skin was so pale that it was almost luminous.

She reached out and touched the scar on my right shoulder. "I gave you this mark a very long time ago."

"You were the one who bit me?" I asked.

"Yes," she replied.

So much for it being a dog bite. It hurt to discover that my father had been lying to me for my entire life. I had no doubt at all that she was telling me the truth. How else could our minds be linked? "Why did you bite me?"

Her lips parted and my eyes were drawn to her teeth. The shadow receded just enough for me to watch as her incisors grew long and sharp. Her grin became something from a horror movie. "Because that is how my kind feeds," she said in a guttural, ravenous voice.

She darted forward and her hands clamped down on my shoulders. My mind went fuzzy when she asserted control over me. She easily stripped away my will, leaving me feeling hollow inside. She pushed my jacket and shirt aside and bit into the old scar. My mouth opened in a silent scream as pain flooded through me. Her bottom teeth grazed my collar bone, but only her top teeth pierced my flesh.

Slurping noisily, she fed deeply and my heart felt as if it was going to burst out of my chest. I knew she was draining me dangerously dry when white spots appeared before my eyes.

Then the light came on and Kala was standing in front of me. Her expression was concerned. "Are you okay?" she asked. "Who turned the light out?"

Putting a hand to my forehead, I tried to clear away the thick fog that had invaded my mind. "I don't know. I didn't see who did it." Something profound had just happened, but I couldn't remember what it was.

"Are you finished in here?"

I couldn't remember whether I'd used the toilet or not, but I didn't feel a pressing need to go. "Yes," I said uncertainly and turned to the basin to wash my hands. They were trembling and my heart was beating far too rapidly. I felt dizzy and strange.

Kala disappeared into one of the stalls. Pain flared in my right shoulder when I reached for a paper towel. Dragging my shirt and jacket away, I saw a slowly healing bite mark directly over the old scar that I'd had since I was a baby. The scar had stretched as I'd grown, but I could tell that the new bite was a match for the old one. There were only faint indentations of a bottom set of teeth on my collarbone. The upper teeth had bitten me savagely enough to tear the flesh and to leave deep bruises.

Staring around wildly, I didn't sense anything dangerous in the restaurant. Something had snuck in, had taken over my mind and had sunk their teeth into me. Somehow, I didn't think this was going to end well. "What the hell is happening to me?" I asked my reflection almost silently.

"Did you say something?" Kala asked as she flushed and exited from the stall.

"I was just wondering if our meals are ready," I said with false brightness.

"I hope they're ready soon," she replied as she washed her hands. "I'm starving."

I smiled in agreement, but my appetite had fled completely. It was hard to think about eating after realizing I'd just been a meal myself for an unknown creature.

Chapter Twenty-Eight

I'd brought my sniper rifle along again with the intention of gunning down the necromancer as soon as I saw him. Mark didn't think our new target was going to waste any time in trying to raise his kin from their entombment. Two people had been reported missing last night, so there was a good chance that the zombie had fed. According to Mark, the necromancer would become whole again once he consumed enough flesh and human blood. That meant his jaw would heal and he'd be able to perform the ritual again.

"If I were the necromancer," Flynn said into the silence, "I'd raise enough corpses to overwhelm us and tear us to pieces." Apparently, I wasn't the only one trying to work out what we could expect from our new foe. "The Zombie King tried it, but he didn't have enough minions to pull it off."

Mark's nod was thoughtful. "I agree. Once night falls, I imagine he'll rise and seek out the closest cemetery. He's probably already healed well enough to speak by now. We need to track him down asap."

We finished our meal quickly and I barely tasted mine. None of us wanted to linger over coffee, so we took to the streets again. There was no point patrolling the cemeteries until dark, so we drove around aimlessly. We all kept watch for Officer Mallory and his partner.

Once the sun began to sink towards the horizon, the tension in the SUV grew. I'd already assembled my rifle. It sat between my knees with the barrel pointing over my shoulder. The safety was on so I wouldn't accidentally shoot anyone in the event that we were involved in a car accident.

Almost as soon as darkness blanketed the city, I felt hidden eyes watching me. I had a brief memory of a woman appearing behind me in the restaurant restroom. Then the picture was gone, hidden behind a mental haze and I forgot about my stalker.

A few minutes later, I sensed a swell of power when the reanimated sorcerer began his spell. I didn't want to think about where he'd gotten the blood that he needed to draw a circle and to mark the graves. "I can feel the necromancer to the north," I told Mark.

The connection between us was faint, which meant he wasn't close by.

Reece put his foot down and surged through the streets, zeroing in on a cemetery that we'd patrolled several times already. We again avoided the cameras rather than shutting them down. Our mission was almost over and we didn't want the local cops involved now.

Green fog permeated the boneyard once again. It stretched to the outer limits of the grounds, almost spilling out onto the street. Everyone but Mark heard a voice chanting and we cautiously moved in closer. Periodically peering through the scope of my rifle, I held up my hand to alert the others when I spotted our target.

Speaking in its native tongue, the necromancer was chanting in an almost hypnotic rhythm. He'd found clothing to cover his nakedness, which I found highly disturbing. He'd regained enough intelligence to realize that he stood out. He was trying to hide the fact that he was a walking corpse. He'd fed well and had regained enough of his jaw to be able to speak. Even his nose was growing back and the hole in his cheek was closing. With a few more meals, he'd be indistinguishable from the living.

I moved in closer and chose a crypt to use as a brace for my rifle. The zombie appeared in my scope again and he turned as he sensed me. With a triumphant grin, he shrieked a final few words and ducked down an instant before I was about to pull the trigger.

"Damn it," I hissed and let the pressure off so I didn't waste the shot. "He knows we're here." Taking him out from a distance was out of the question now. He was already scurrying away as crypts and mausoleums exploded and dozens of corpses came back to life.

The necromancer had put far more energy into this mass resurrection. His minions were so fresh that they almost looked alive. Once they began to move, it was obvious they were far from normal. Their steps were hesitant and they lurched rather than walked. Moaning in hunger, they shambled towards us as more and more graves broke open.

Hiding behind a crypt, the necromancer hissed a command and half of the newly risen broke off to follow him. The rest continued to move towards us, intent on feeding.

"Form a circle," Mark ordered and we complied. I was on his left and Flynn was on his right. Kala and Reece were at our backs. My flamethrower was slung over my left shoulder. I put my sniper rifle on the ground at my feet and reached for my other weapon. I flicked the safety off and pulled the trigger as a zombie came within range. It gave a buzzing mental and verbal shriek as a twenty foot flame shot out to engulf it.

It quickly grew hot with flames intermittently flaring to take down the ravenous creatures. I armed sweat away and sent another blast flying. Mindless with hunger and following their master's command, they climbed over the bodies of the fallen to get to us. Their ability to recognize danger had been crushed beneath the weight of their order to kill us.

By the time we finished off the last of the walking dead, I was almost out of fuel. Kala shook her canister to hear nothing sloshing around inside. "That was a close one," she breathed.

Mark wiped sweat away from his forehead with his handkerchief. His hand was shaking when he pulled his cell phone out of his pocket. He called for the Cleanup Crew and I didn't envy them their job this night. Over a hundred bodies lay smoldering on the ground. Nearly the same number had gotten away from us.

"We might need to call in reinforcements," our boss said when he turned in a circle to survey the battle scene.

All three of my fellow shifters instantly scowled. "We can handle this," Reece said.

Kala pointed in the direction where the necromancer and his minions had fled. "We'll follow them on foot and you can catch up to us in the SUV." We were far faster than the newly risen. We should be able to find them quickly enough.

"How much fuel do you have left?" he asked. Almost all of our canisters were empty and we needed to restock. Reaching his decision, Mark jerked his head for us to follow him. "You need to restock first."

I knew the PIA had other teams working for them, but I knew very little about them. It was obvious that the Shifter Squad believed they were superior to their human contemporaries and that we didn't require any help. Personally, I thought a few extra guns would come in handy right about now. I snatched up my rifle and hurried after the others.

Reaching the SUV, we each took a fresh flamethrower. Flynn shoved extra canisters into a duffle bag then slung it over his shoulder.

Reece addressed Mark. "Kala will keep in touch with you and Lexi while we hunt them down."

"I don't think so," I said. No way was I going to sit this one out.

He turned to me and stared down his nose arrogantly. "I'm the team leader and you'll follow my orders."

"I'm the only one who can sense them if you lose their trail, oh great and mighty Team Leader," I said with heavy sarcasm.

Flynn was brave enough to come to my rescue. "She has a point."

"We don't have time to argue," Mark said impatiently. "You can't treat Alexis like a porcelain doll, Agent Garrett. She's tougher than you think."

Brown eyes a few shades lighter than mine scrutinized me, then Reece shrugged his shoulders in capitulation. "Fine," he ground out unhappily. "Let's move out."

Kala and Flynn fell in behind him and I brought up the rear. We ran back through the cemetery and picked up the stench of zombie and followed it to the far side of the grounds. The undead had swarmed over the wall rather than using the gate. We leaped over it as well and went in pursuit.

Chapter Twenty-Nine

Leaving both the graveyard and residential neighborhoods behind us, we entered an industrial area. We followed the trail for several blocks, then found ourselves at the edge of the city. "I can sense them just ahead," I whispered and we slowed down. Dawn wasn't far away and a low mist was beginning to rise.

We came to a fence that bordered a boggy marsh. It had been knocked down by stampeding zombies. We cleared the wire in a single bound. Far across the field, we saw our quarry approaching a stand of trees. Half a dozen old buildings stood off to one side. The remains of a sign had been propped up against a wall. I did a double-take when I read the word 'Billings -ter Ya-'. The rest of the sign was obscured by mud.

"We need to catch up to them before the sun rises and they burrow beneath the ground," Reece said and we hastened forward.

The sign bothered me, but I couldn't figure out why. As we closed in on the small army of undead, the necromancer glanced back and saw us. Gleeful malice sparkled in eyes that were now a clear brown rather than milky. I wished I'd brought my rifle, but I'd left it in the back of the SUV.

Smelling fresh blood, I glanced down to see that we were approaching a ritual circle. With a dry chuckle, the necromancer sprang his trap. Uttering the last words of his spell that he must have begun before we'd arrived, he called forth a very different type of army.

Long dead cows, pigs and sheep spewed out of the earth all around us. Their bones must have been tossed into a mass grave decades ago.

"Am I really seeing this?" Flynn said in a horrified tone.

"I hope not," Kala replied. "Because if you're seeing it, then that means I'm seeing it, too."

The necromancer had used just enough power to restore the animals to a state of quasi-life. Emaciated and almost fleshless, their skin hung from their bodies. Their bones showed up starkly through holes in their hides. Hollow sockets, where their eyes should have been, gaped darkly. Blindly sensing that food was within their reach, they lurched and stumbled towards us with moos, oinks and baas of hunger. I realized now that the sign must have read 'Billings Slaughter Yard'.

My fear and loathing of the undead didn't extend to these things. Maybe because their thoughts weren't battering at my mind. My hands twitched on my weapon from my need to kill them. Thousands of the horrors crowded the field, barring our way. We didn't have enough fuel to kill them all.

"What are we going to do?" I asked.

Reece had already made a decision. "We'll have to lead them away from town until dawn. They'll have to seek shelter from the sun then."

It would have been easy enough for us to outdistance the pursuing herd of zombie animals, but that wasn't our goal. Saving our fuel for when it would be needed, we headed away from New Orleans. Using ourselves as bait, we led the hungry mob like pied pipers. Kala called Mark to tell him about our plan. She warned him to keep his distance so he didn't accidentally lead any of the animals astray.

The reanimated herd converged on anything that was unwise enough to show itself. Each meal restored them a little, but it would take a lot more than the occasional squirrel or fox to fully flesh them out.

After half an hour or so of leading them into the marsh as deep we could go without sinking, the sun finally came up. Letting out harsh bellows of frustration, the animals sank into the ground, leaving no signs of disrupted dirt behind. My mind shied away from the catastrophe that awaited come nightfall when the herd would rise again.

Mark parked the SUV as close to the field as he could get and followed Kala's directions to reach us. His shoes and pants were filthy when he finally reached us. I looked down to see that my cargo pants and sneakers were in the same poor condition. "How many of them are there?" he asked.

"Thousands," Reece replied. "Too many for us to handle alone." The admission cost him and he received sympathetic grimaces from Kala and Flynn.

Agent Steel surveyed the field, noting the size of the area. "We might not have to call in outside help just yet."

A mischievous grin appeared on Kala's mouth. "What are you planning, boss?"

"We have a weapon in the compound that should be able to wipe out all of the animals when they rise. I think there should be enough of the stuff."

"I thought fire was the best way to kill them," I said in confusion.

"Oh, we'll be using fire," Mark confirmed. "We're just going to need a different type of fuel to eradicate this many targets. Reece, Flynn, make sure no one approaches the area. Girls, I'll need your help to load up the SUV."

The two guys nodded, looking as alert as ever. We'd been up all night and now that we'd stopped leading the herd away from the city, I realized that I was unusually exhausted. I trailed behind Mark and Kala, almost stumbling in my tiredness.

It was a relief to sink down onto the backseat. For a change, I had the whole seat to myself. I stretched out, being careful to keep my muddy shoes off the upholstery. My nose wrinkled at the stench of marshy soil then I leaned my head back and dropped off to sleep.

"Lexi, we're here." I started awake when I heard my name and stared at Kala uncomprehendingly. I'd been in the middle of a nightmare about being stalked by a strange and frightening woman. "Are you feeling okay?" she asked in concern.

Shaking my head in an effort to clear it, I offered her a weak smile. "I'm a bit tired," I admitted. I was terribly thirsty and felt as if I hadn't slept in a week and I wondered what was wrong with me.

Mark had already climbed out of the SUV. He waited impatiently for us at the door. "Let's get a move on, ladies."

"Aye, aye, Captain," Kala said and snapped him a salute. I smiled at her hijinks, but couldn't quite dredge up a laugh. Exhaustion was still sucking at me, trying to drag me back to sleep.

Leaving our flamethrowers in the back of the vehicle, we followed him down the long hallway to where the weapons were stored. Mark scanned his palm to open the door and we filed inside. We moved past the empty pegs where our flamethrowers usually hung and headed to the far end of the long stretch of cupboards. Mark hunkered down, opened a door and pulled out a bright red five gallon container. Strain showed on his face as he handed it to Kala. Liquid sloshed inside. It must be the mysterious fuel he'd spoken of.

Rolling her eyes, she passed it to me and motioned for him to move aside. "Why don't you let me do that? I wouldn't want you to pull a muscle," she said sweetly.

Conceding that she had greater strength than he did, he stood and used his handkerchief to mop his brow. "How many do we need?" she asked as she knelt down to grab the next container.

Calculating the size of the field and the number of monsters that we'd be facing, he shrugged. "We'd better take all of it." He was adopting an attitude that it was better to have too much than too little.

I ducked down to see red containers stretching out to both sides. "How many containers are there?"

"Thirty," Mark said with a bland expression.

I could see why he needed our help and hefted the next container that Kala handed to me. While we managed to carry four apiece, Mark struggled to carry two. He set one down to open the door for us.

Far quicker than he'd have been able to manage on his own, we had the SUV loaded up. There was barely enough room to hold all of the containers. We had to rest some of them on the backseat and the floor. Kala and I cradled two containers on our laps as we headed back to the field.

My tiredness grew worse as we slogged across the field carrying an armful of containers. Reece and Flynn jogged over to the SUV to assist us with the heavy lifting. Mark oversaw the operation as we poured the liquid as evenly as we could across the entire field. He made sure that every scrap of ground was soaked in the acrid smelling fuel. The moment night fell, the herd would rise and would become coated in the liquid. One small burst of flame should be enough to turn them all into roast meals.

Chapter Thirty

It took us hours to empty all of the containers. We were starving by the time we were done.

"Can we get some food?" Kala complained. "We haven't eaten since last night." Hers wasn't the only stomach grumbling. Strangely, I felt less hungry than I should have. I was too exhausted to worry about eating.

We were all filthy from head to toe and we weren't in any condition to enter a restaurant. "Wait here," Mark said. "Lexi and I will grab some takeaway."

"You don't look so good," Flynn said to me. "Are you feeling all right?" That was the second time I'd been asked that question and I wondered just how bad I looked.

"I'm fine," I lied. "I just need some sleep."

Leaving the team at the edge of the deadly field, Mark and I climbed back into the SUV. "What's wrong with you?" he asked as soon as we were too far away for the others to be able to overhear us.

"I don't know," I replied honestly. "I'm just really, really tired." New Orleans was hot and humid and we kept bottled water in the vehicle. I cracked open a bottle and drank down a few mouthfuls.

He snatched quick glances at my face as he drove towards the city. "You're very pale. Maybe you need more iron in your diet."

I'd never suffered from an iron deficiency before, but anything was possible. I made a noncommittal sound and we lapsed into silence. Unused to eating takeaway so often, I asked for a semi-healthy salad rather than a burger and fries. While Mark waited for our order to be filled, I took a trip to the restroom.

When I was done, I felt a sense of trepidation as I washed my hands at the sink. My stomach fluttered nervously and I kept glancing in the mirror, expecting someone, or some*thing* to pop up behind me. Nothing did and I escaped from the room safely. I was mystified as to why I had been afraid at all.

My eyes tried to slide shut during the drive back to the field, but I snapped awake each time. I was reluctant to slide back into the nightmare of being hunted by an unknown pursuer.

"Food!" Kala cried happily when we pulled to a stop beside the team. We'd only passed a few cars on the way to and from the field. We were in an area that had been almost utterly devastated by Katrina years ago. Few had tried to rebuild their homes here and the land was largely deserted. We couldn't have picked a better place to face the horde come nightfall.

"Just how flammable is that stuff?" Flynn asked after he'd finished his meal. He hiked his thumb at the stinky field that was coated in the oily looking substance.

"Extremely," Mark said dryly. "There's a good chance they'll be able to see the flames from outer space."

"You're joking, right?" I said, suddenly feeling much more awake. We'd been as careful as possible when splashing the stuff around, but our shoes and lower pants were soaked in it.

"Not even a little bit," he replied seriously. "That's why I'll need you all to stand well clear when I set the field on fire." He'd stayed at a safe distance back as he'd directed us to coat the ground. Mark was the only one who wasn't a walking incendiary device waiting to happen.

There were still a couple of hours left before the sun would fall from the sky and Reece pointed at the SUV. "You're exhausted. Why don't you try to get some rest before the bonfire starts?"

I opened my mouth to protest, but Mark seized on the idea. "I agree. You need sleep. We'll wake you before the action begins."

It was useless to argue, so I trudged over to the vehicle and climbed inside. It stank of fumes already and I didn't want to make matters worse. I slid my shoes off and left them on the ground. Next, I rolled my pants up so the dirt wouldn't smear the seats. The backseat wasn't long enough for me to stretch out, so I tucked my knees up when I lay down.

Closing my eyes, I instantly dropped off to sleep and was hurtled backwards into a long forgotten memory.

Looking upwards, I stared in wonder at the objects that floated above me. I was too young to know that it was a mobile of the moon and stars. All sights and sounds were strange and mysterious to me. A noise had woken me, but I wasn't sure what it was. A soft light lit the room well enough for me to see a shadow when it moved into the doorway. It stood there for a while, just watching me before it entered the room.

Primitive fear filled my tiny body as the shadow fell over me and pale hands reached down to pick me up. Used to being treated gently and with care, I let out a startled cry when the hands bruised my flesh in a tight grip. A wide, grinning mouth was all I saw before teeth tore into my flesh. Screaming in agony, I struggled uselessly as my blood was drained away and my vision began to go dark. My father appeared in the doorway and I held my hand out to him beseechingly. Bright light flared and a loud noise rang out. It hurt my ears and dampened all other sound.

A hand touched my knee and I woke with a scream. Knocking the hand away, my heart thudded in my chest in terror. Flynn started back in surprise at my reaction. Kala caught him before he could sprawl to the ground. Reece's face came into view behind them. All three stared at me in concern. My shoulder was throbbing. It felt as if I'd just been bitten moments ago rather than when I was an infant.

"Did I hear a scream?" Mark called from his position near the field. The sun was about to go down and we didn't have time to discuss my nightmare.

"I'm fine," I called back. "It was just a bad dream." My hoarse voice was a telltale sign that I was lying, but he let it go.

Kala offered me her hand and I took it. She pulled me upright and I slid to the edge of the seat to don my shoes. "What were you dreaming about?" she asked me curiously.

"I think I was remembering being bitten by the dog when I was a baby." In my dream, it hadn't been a dog at all, but something far more terrifying. The dream was already beginning to fade and it would soon be gone. I wasn't sad to see it go.

"Don't worry," Flynn said with a grin. "We won't let any of these zombie beasts bite you."

It was logical to assume I was dreaming about being bitten because we were about to confront thousands of undead cows, pigs and sheep. I didn't think our coming battle was the real cause of my nightmare, but I wasn't sure what had sparked it.

Folding my pants back down, I took the fully loaded flamethrower that Reece handed me and took up a spot beside the others. We stood across the road, waiting for the last rays of sunlight to fade from the sky. A nervous energy spread through our ranks, waking me up a little. Mark stood only fifteen feet from the edge of what would shortly become a killing field.

Our tension grew and I sensed the zombies awaken. "Any second now," I whispered. A moment after I spoke, the ground erupted and the skeletal horde spilled from their resting places. Mark didn't hesitate. He sent a burst of flame at the ground. Instantly, a conflagration sprang into being. He was thrown backward as the fiery shockwave spread across the entire field.

Reece dropped his weapon and sprinted across the road. He snatched our boss into his arms and tossed him over his shoulder. He raced to safety before the heat of the flames could ignite their clothing. Reece was lucky his pants and shoes hadn't caught on fire. If Mark hadn't been thrown backwards a few feet, they probably would have.

Mark hadn't exaggerated about the intensity of the fire. Shielding my face from the brightness, I squinted through the gaps in my fingers to see the animals burning merrily. In seconds, the flames had captured every zombie in its greedy clutches. Screams and bellows of agony were drowned out beneath the crackle of the fire that shot a full forty feet into the air.

Coughing and gasping for air, Mark sat down on the side of the road and watched the horde burn.

"Well," he said after he'd regained his breath. "I'd say the fuel worked." Steam was wafting off him, signaling just how close he'd come to being roasted along with the beasts.

Kala sniggered, then I sniggered and even Flynn's shoulders moved in silent laughter. Reece sent us a disapproving glare that did nothing to dampen our mirth. We all knew we'd come close to losing Mark and this was our way of dealing with the stress.

It only took a few minutes for the herd to burn to ash. With them gone, I detected the other zombies that had risen with nightfall. The necromancer wasn't sticking around to watch the bonfire. He and his minions were already on their way back towards town.

"The necromancer is on the move," I warned the others.

"Which direction are they heading in?" Mark asked and gestured for us to climb into the SUV. It had been parked a little too close to the fire and some of the black paint had blistered.

"Towards the city."

"Of course they are," Kala scowled. "They need food and they'll chow down on the first humans that they come across."

"Then we'd better haul butt and catch them," Mark said gravely.

Chapter Thirty-One

Travelling by car meant that we were restricted to following the roads. We lost ground and Reece had to put his foot down. We had to move fast to have a hope of catching up to our targets as they cut across the fields to the industrial area on the outskirts of the city.

Leaning forward, I pointed at a large group of shadowy figures that were clumsily sprinting along the side of the road ahead.

"I see them," Reece said and the SUV surged forward.

We were almost on them when the necromancer glanced backwards and grinned craftily. He lifted his hand as a signal and his band of merry men and women disappeared beneath the ground.

"They're like undead moles," Kala complained. She and Flynn were squeezed in beside me so they could see the action through the windscreen as well.

"Where did they go?" I asked.

"They can only resurface somewhere they've already been before," Mark said.

Flynn had a theory about where that would be. "If I were the necromancer, I'd head to one of the cemeteries and start raising more soldiers."

"Which cemetery?" Kala asked.

"Weren't his minions all made at the graveyard where he killed the Zombie King?" I pointed out.

Mark nodded. "You're right. That's the only cemetery they'll be able to reach quickly."

"How fast can they move underground?" Kala queried.

"They can disappear and reappear almost instantly," was his disturbing answer. "It's a phenomenon that has only ever been seen with zombies. We believe it has something to do with the death magic that animates them."

That was disturbing, yet it was also a relief. I couldn't imagine facing a wide range of enemies that could disappear at will.

Knowing the city well by now, we headed for the cemetery and parked a short distance away.

"We're too late," Flynn said in despair when we saw the telltale signs of green fog beginning to spread out.

"Not quite," I replied. "The necromancer must still be working on his spell. I can only sense the original hundred or so."

Kala shook her head as she pushed her door open "How bad do things have to be if we think that a hundred zombies is a small number?"

Armed with flamethrowers and spare canisters of fuel, we hurried towards the small side gate that wasn't being watched by cameras. We snuck up as close as we could get to the circle of undead corpses that were guarding their master. The Cleanup Crew had removed all evidence of our battle from last night, including the body of the Zombie King. I didn't really care where his remains had been interred, just as long as they were far away from here. It hurt my brain to think of the bokor dying and then being reanimated by the necromancer that he himself had turned into a zombie.

The zombies had snatched up a human on their way to the cemetery. A woman's crumpled body lay discarded on the ground. Her head was missing. The necromancer had repeated his act with his master and had cracked her skull open. He was flicking blood and brains onto the ground as he walked his unholy circle, chanting his spell.

A sixth sense warned him that danger was near. He looked beyond his guardians and through the misty fog straight at me. The miasma was becoming thicker by the second and it would soon obscure our quarry completely. Knowing he was running out of time, he walked the rest of his circle, chanting faster.

"We need to stop him before he completes the ritual," Reece said and barely waited for Mark's nod before he leaped forward.

The rest of us were right behind him. We spread out into a line as the undead guardians hissed in warning and moved to surround us. Bright orange flames shot from our weapons, turning the zombies into screaming torches.

"Lexi," Mark shouted over the noise. "I need you to target the necromancer. If you kill him, his minions will be confused and they'll hopefully stop attacking us in force."

I shouldered the flamethrower and reached for my Beretta. Shuffling quickly, the necromancer threw a frantic look over his shoulder and ducked when I pulled the trigger. My bullet just grazed the top of his head and he bellowed in rage and fright.

Ignoring the battle that was going on around me, I tracked his movements and fired again. My second bullet slammed into his head, blowing a large hole out the other side. Rotting brains stained the white marble of a crypt. He screeched shrilly and the mob of walking corpses that were attacking us hesitated and looked around in confusion.

If he'd been human, the wound would have killed him. Since he was undead, it would take a lot more than one bullet to finish him off. He'd neared the end of his spell and the fog had thickened to the point where I could barely see him. I sensed that he was seconds away from raising far more than just a couple of hundred corpses as he began chanting again.

"I have to get closer," I said to the others and darted into the fog before anyone could stop me.

Cursing, Reece fired at a group of walking dead, then raced after me as I dodged the oncoming enemies.

With a last few steps and sprinkling of blood and brains scooped from the dead woman's skull, the necromancer completed his spell with a triumphant shout. A shockwave of power swept out, nearly knocking me off my feet. Reece stumbled, then righted himself. We stood back to back as hundreds of reanimated corpses spilled from their graves. These zombies had been hastily formed and were in a pitiful condition. The stench of decomposing flesh made me want to gag.

"There's too many of them," my protector said in a tone that sounded calm on the surface. Tied to his mind, I knew that he was afraid. The Shifter Squad was fierce and powerful, but even we couldn't take on this many ravenous zombies and hope to live.

"If we're going down, I'm taking the necromancer with us," I vowed.

Reading my mind, he smiled in pure pleasure. "I've got your back, Agent Levine."

Spying the necromancer inching away, I sprang into action. Our only advantage over the horde was our speed. We dodged, ducked and weaved our way through the throng until I was close enough to see my target clearly. His eyes widened in terror when he saw my resolve. In mid-run, I lifted my gun and sent four rapid shots at him.

All four bullets hit their mark and the necromancer's head exploded in a wash of black brains and clotted, noisome blood. Roars of rage issued from hundreds of zombie throats as their master fell. I closed the distance between us to see the necromancer still stubbornly clinging to life.

Kicking him over onto his back, I struggled against the urge to gag again when I saw that only part of his head was still left intact. One eye glared up at me, his other eye was gone, along with most of his skull.

"What are you?" he asked in heavily accented English.

"I'm a werewolf," I replied truthfully.

Staring up at me, his hands scrabbled at the ground and I wondered if he was in pain. The thought came with no guilt. He was the enemy and it was my job to kill him. "No," he said feebly. "You are more than that. You are like me."

Reece was at my back, shooting warning bursts of fire at the approaching army. He sent me a startled look over his shoulder.

"I'm nothing like you," I argued. "I'm not a zombie."

"Yet, you are not fully alive," he countered. "It would not take much to turn you into my kind completely." He turned thoughtful, then began to chant in a low, almost hypnotic voice.

His mind began to invade mine, trying to compel me to submit to him. I had a strong sense of déjà vu, as if someone else had recently tried to bend me to their will. Cringing inwardly at the slimy mental probing, I pointed my gun at his face. "I don't think so," I said coldly and pumped half a dozen rounds into what was left of his head.

A sigh went out through the army as their leader became an inert corpse again. As one, they turned to me. Instead of attacking, it almost seemed as if they were waiting for instructions. The echoes of the link that had briefly tied me to the necromancer still remained. Acting on impulse, I address the waiting minions. "Go back to your resting places and return to death's embrace," I ordered them.

I was astonished and relieved when they turned and began making their way back to their crypts.

"Do I even want to know how you did that?" Reece asked.

"I wish I knew," I lied. I wasn't ready to confess that I was tied to the undead just as I was linked to him, if far less strongly. It was a wonder that he couldn't sense them through me.

"Wait here," he instructed. "I'm going to check on the others."

Clearly, he wanted to put some distance between us so he could think about what he'd just seen. I nodded again and leaned back against a crypt. Stinking of gas fumes, ash and roasted zombie, I was drained of energy and was ready to sleep for a week.

Sensing eyes on me, I turned my head to see a pale woman standing only a few feet away. There was something familiar about her, but I couldn't quite put my finger on it.

"At last, we are alone," she said. The green mist and shadows worked together to hide her face from me, but I knew I'd heard her voice before. Her accent was foreign, most likely European.

"Do I know you?" I had a sense of déjà vu again. It was even stronger this time. I tried to back away when she reached for me, but I was trapped by the crypt.

"Oh yes," she said with a tinkling laugh that was jarring to my ears. "You might say that we are very close. Or we were once." She put one hand on my left shoulder and pulled me towards her. "I hope that we will soon be closer than ever before." I was helpless to resist her when she tugged my shirt and jacket aside and bit into my right shoulder. I made a sound of pain, but she had control of my mind and commanded me to be silent.

I heard a voice calling my name and blinked in confusion. "Lexi?" the voice called again. It was Reece and he sounded concerned.

For a moment, I had no idea where I was. Then I saw that I was surrounded by graves and remembered that we'd been hunting the necromancer. Turning, I stumbled and had to catch myself on a crypt. "I'm here," I croaked.

Hearing me, Reece ran to my side. "Are you all right?" he asked, searching the area for a threat.

Clammy and feeling faint, I shook my head. "I don't feel very good."

"What happened?" He took my hand and some of my strength returned just from his simple touch.

"I don't know. I don't remember."

"I was worried when I suddenly couldn't feel you again."

"What do you mean?" I was having trouble concentrating on his words.

"Something happened to the bond," he explained. "I felt it growing weaker and weaker until I couldn't sense you at all. This is the second time this has happened."

I had no idea what he was talking about at first, then realized what he meant. I could feel him, but the connection was faint. I'd wanted the bond gone, but I had no idea what was causing it to weaken like this. Whatever it was, it was making me feel weak as well. "When was the first time this happened?"

"When you took a bathroom break in the restaurant."

I vaguely remembered feeling disquieted at the time, but couldn't recall why. Before I could ponder on the puzzle, the others caught up to us. Mark sent me a sharp glance. "What's wrong?"

"Lexi isn't feeling well," Reece replied. "We should get her back to the base."

"You're very pale," Kala said as she slipped my arm over her shoulder. She and Reece helped me back to the SUV.

Mark had already called the Cleanup Crew and their van arrived just as we were leaving. I still wasn't sure how I'd managed to make the corpses return to their graves, but the Crew wouldn't have the laborious task of disposing of quite so many undead this time.

I fell into a semi doze once I was inside the SUV. My head lolled on Kala's shoulder and she put her arm around my waist.

Flynn took my hand. "She's so cold," he murmured and then I blacked out.

When I woke, it was morning and I was in my room. I was dressed in a t-shirt and undies and I didn't remember putting them on. I couldn't remember much of what had happened the night before, which was frightening. Something strange was going on and I didn't know what it was.

I took a long, hot shower and toweled my hair dry. Staring at my reflection while I ran a brush through my hair, the scar on my right shoulder caught my eye. It looked different somehow and I leaned in close to see it. Instead of the old, faded teeth marks, it looked almost new. My blood ran cold when I realized that I'd been bitten by something and that I didn't remember it. Then I was confused because hadn't I already had this thought before?

Dressing, I went downstairs for breakfast and found the others sitting at the table. Mark smiled, but it was strained. "How are you feeling?" he asked. I had the feeling they'd been talking about me.

"Tired," I replied and turned to Kala. "Did you help me get changed last night?" I hoped it'd been her. If it was any of the others, I'd die of embarrassment.

"Help you?" she scoffed. "You were completely unconscious. It was like dressing a life-sized doll." She shuddered slightly in remembrance.

"Do you remember what happened last night in the cemetery?" Mark asked me.

I shrugged while I poured milk into my cereal. "Some of it. It's all a bit hazy."

He was silent for a moment while I crossed to the table and took a seat. The whole team was subdued. It almost seemed as if they were afraid for me. Or of me. I couldn't tell which.

"I'd like you to take another trip into the city to see the voodoo priestess," he said.

I paused with my spoon halfway to my mouth. "Why?"

"I'd like you to ask her if we've eliminated the threat from the Zombie King and the necromancer."

"Why do you want me to ask her?" I asked, narrowing my eyes with suspicion.

"Because she'd only talk to you the last time," he pointed out.

I didn't feel up to a trip, but it would be churlish to refuse his request. "Okay," I said with a shrug and pushed my bowl away. I'd barely touched my cereal, but I wasn't hungry. All I wanted to do was sleep.

"Reece will drive you to New Orleans this afternoon," Mark said and stood. He headed for the coms room before I could muster up a protest that I could drive myself. I swayed on my feet when I stood and had to revise that thought. Maybe it wasn't such a bad idea to have a chauffeur after all.

Chapter Thirty-Two

I intended to spend the day reading through the archives, but I spent most of my time dozing instead. I woke when a fist banged on my bedroom door.

"Lexi!" Reece shouted. "Are you ready to go?"

"I'll meet you downstairs in five minutes!" I shouted back. My legs were wobbly when I entered the bathroom. Checking my reflection, I winced at what I saw. Dark circles crouched beneath my eyes and my cheeks were hollow. I'd already been thin, but I'd lost weight and was beginning to look ill. "What's wrong with me?" I asked the girl in the mirror, but she didn't respond.

Changing into jeans, a tank top, my holster and my red leather jacket, I checked that my gun wasn't visible before leaving my room. There was no need for my rifle and I left it tucked away in the closet. Hopefully, we wouldn't need the flamethrowers that were still stashed in the back of the SUV.

Reece waited for me to buckle myself in before triggering the button that opened the garage door. I closed my eyes to rest for a moment and when I opened them again, we were entering New Orleans.

"Are you awake?" Reece asked. His tone was ragged and I wondered what I'd done to annoy him this time.

"Yes." Barely. I'd spent the whole day sleeping, yet I still felt inexplicably drained of energy.

We parked outside the voodoo store and Reece had my door open even before I'd unbuckled the seatbelt. I was as slow and clumsy as an ordinary human and it made me irritable. He ignored my glare and helped me out of the SUV.

I hated to admit it, but I seemed to gain some strength from his touch as he guided me inside the store with a hand on my elbow. The bell jingled as we entered. The voodoo priestess glanced up, saw me and froze. She made a sound of horror and rushed out from behind the counter. "I feared this," she said as she checked my eyes and then my pulse.

"Feared what?" my concerned companion asked. "Do you know what's wrong with her?"

The priestess flicked a glance at him, then addressed me. "I warned you that your spirit was at war."

"I remember," I said and talking was hard. "I didn't really understand what you were talking about." I still didn't and hoped that she was about to enlighten me. Maybe she'd have a solution for whatever was wrong with me.

"The battle that is raging inside you is tearing you apart," she said. "You must take steps to defend yourself, or you will lose your soul to the darkness."

I still had no idea what she was talking about and my expression reflected my confusion.

"What does she have to do?" Reece asked. He stood at my back with a hand on my left shoulder. His palm rested on the mark that he'd given me. It seemed to pulse beneath his hand.

"You must strengthen the bond between you in order to break the hold that the darkness has over her."

I didn't like the sounds of that. "How?"

"You know how," she chided, as if I was being deliberately obtuse. "There is only one way to make your bond stronger."

Unwillingly, I turned so I could see Reece's expression. He stared down at me with an inscrutable look, but I sensed his flare of anticipation before he dampened it.

"You must do this before the sun is gone from the sky," the priestess warned us.

"Did we destroy the zombie threat?" I asked. That was what Mark had sent us here to discover, not to listen to some mystical mumbo jumbo about my soul.

"There is only one soulless left in this city now," she said darkly. "And it is not a zombie." She knew what it was, but she wasn't going to elaborate.

Reece guided me back outside and over to the SUV. I climbed inside and couldn't bring myself to look at him as he drove through the city. Instead of heading back to the compound, he pulled up outside a hotel.

Too tired to ask him why we were stopping, I watched him climb out and walk to the back of the SUV. He opened the back door and covered the flamethrowers with a blanket. Then he was opening my door and was helping me out. We stepped into the hotel and headed over to the reception desk. In a slight daze, I listened without protest as he used his credit card to pay for a room for the night.

It didn't occur to me that he was taking the priestess' advice seriously until we were standing in the bedroom and he was taking his clothes off.

"What are you doing?" I asked him in alarm.

"You heard the priestess," he replied evenly. "We have to strengthen the bond or you'll lose your soul."

I heard a hint of sarcasm in his tone and crossed my arms. "You don't really believe that."

Stripping his t-shirt off, he dropped it to the floor then moved to stand in front of me. "I'm not sure what to believe. All I know is that you're sick and that I might be able to help you."

"By having sex with me," I said flatly.

"If that's what it takes." He read the anguish in my eyes and sighed. "I know what you're thinking. That I'm only doing this because I have no choice."

"Aren't you?" We hadn't had any choice the last two times we'd been naked together. Why should this time be any different?

"Can we talk about this later?" he asked and took a step closer.

This might not be his choice, but I felt his desire tickling the back of my mind. We hadn't even touched each other yet and the bond was already growing stronger. My gaze dropped from his face to his chest and swept down to his sculpted abs. I remembered what it felt like to have his hands on me and I swayed towards him. His hands enclosed my shoulders and he bent to kiss me.

For a long moment, I resisted the feelings that rose up to engulf me. Then I was on my tippy toes and my hands were clutching Reece's shoulders, trying to pull him closer. My jacket dropped to the floor and my tank top and jeans followed. He stripped his pants off without breaking contact with me then he picked me up and pulled my legs around his waist. He sat on the edge of the bed with me on his lap. I looked down at his obvious arousal and blushed bright red. This was the first time that neither of us had been under the influence of mind control. We knew exactly what we were doing and we would remember every moment of it when we were done.

He laughed silently and pulled me closer. "It's too late for modesty, Alexis. I've seen you naked before and I've already been inside you." His hands moved from my back to my butt and he slid me up and down his body slowly. "You rode me like this in the back of that car." His voice was thick with desire and something deep inside me clenched in response.

I didn't protest when he undid my bra and slid it down my arms. I was beyond being able to call a halt to this. Deep down inside, I admitted that I didn't want him to stop. I wanted him inside me again.

Now with only my undies between us, I leaned forward until my breasts were brushing his chest. I kissed him deeply and had a flash of memory of doing this exact thing once before. His thumb brushed against the most intimate part of me and I moaned into his mouth.

In a swift move that made my head spin, he had me on my back and was lying on top of me. Our lips melded, our tongues touched and the heat began to build. Reece swept a hand down my side and back up to cup my breast. "You're so beautiful," he breathed into my neck then slid down my torso and took my nipple into his mouth.

Lost in sensation, I gripped a handful of sheets when he moved even lower and kissed his way down my body. He paused to slip my undies off, then simply gazed at my body. His hands were resting on my thighs and I didn't have the strength or the will to resist him when he nudged them apart. His head dipped, his tongue touched me and my body convulsed in response.

When I didn't think I could take it any longer, he guided himself inside me and plunged in deep. A moan escaped me and was swallowed when we kissed. My legs went around his and my hands slid down to his lower back when he began to move. With each stroke, the heat built up and the bond strengthened.

I sensed the same heat within Reece, then our minds became more fully entwined than they'd ever been before. Like a dam bursting, I remembered the night that Lust had taken control of me. I saw it through both his memory and mine as he pounded himself inside me. I recalled his astonishment and pleasure as I'd ridden him and his guilt when we'd reached our peak.

He had the same revelation of when he'd been forced to seek me out due to the telepath's command. He remembered our first night together, the night that he'd taken my virginity. "I *was* your first," he murmured with profound satisfaction and an emotion that could only be classed as possession. He'd already figured this was the case, but now there could be no doubt.

Before I could speak, more memories came back to me. This time, they had nothing to do with compulsion and everything to do with my alter ego. In excruciating detail, I remembered the first time I'd changed into a werewolf. That memory paled in comparison to the second time I'd become a monster. I remembered hunting down the zombies that had invaded my territory. I saw Mark as the pitifully small and weak human being that he was and I saw myself carrying him back to the prison where my mate was being kept. Most of all, I remembered my link to Reece.

Together, we relived the three nights that we'd spent in his enclosure. We'd felt joy in the hunt and peace at being a pack. In our half-wolf forms, we knew we were destined to be together. Everything was simple when we didn't have human emotions to complicate everything.

Teeth lightly grazed my left shoulder without breaking the skin and I was brought back to the here and now. If Reece switched sides, he might see the fresh mark at the back of my right shoulder. The thought was almost enough to jolt me from my pleasure.

"I'm the only man who has ever done this to you," he said as he increased his thrusts to a frantic pace. "I'm the only one who will ever be inside your body." He lifted his head and stared down at me. "Say it," he demanded in a hoarse voice. His eyes were a shade lighter than usual, as if he was close to his change.

We were both alphas, but in that moment, his will was stronger than mine. "I'm yours," I whispered and triumph blazed from his eyes. The heat became unbearable, then I was hurtling over the edge, taking him with me as my body bucked in pleasure.

Lying on top of me, Reece fought to get his breath back, then rolled onto his side. Our bond had been restored, but he clamped down on his emotions so tightly that I couldn't sense them. "The bond has been repaired, so your soul should be safe from whatever darkness the voodoo priestess was talking about," he said calmly and as if he hadn't just claimed my body forever.

Still tingling all over, I knew instinctively that my promise had been just as binding as the marks on our shoulders. I knew little about alphas and shifters in general, but I sensed through our link that I had become his.

Pushing my newfound knowledge behind a wall in my mind to hide it from him, I nodded and pulled the sheet up to my chin. "At least we know I'm not pregnant now," I replied. In our shifted forms, we'd hunted, played and slept, but we hadn't mated. Our bond had been too new to start a family. I wasn't carrying a bellyful of puppies and my relief was almost strong enough to reduce me to tears.

Climbing out of bed, Reece didn't look at me as he dressed. "I'll call Mark and tell him that we'll be back soon."

"I'm going to take a shower," I said, trying to pretend that I wasn't falling apart on the inside.

Nodding, he pulled his phone out of his pocket and stepped outside.

Alone in the room, I slid out of bed and gathered up my clothes. I took my second shower for the day and silent sobs wracked me from head to toe. Once again, Reece had done his duty. We were members of the same pack and he was compelled to keep me safe, even if that meant he had to sacrifice his body again. While he'd tried hard to hide his emotions from me, I sensed his anguish at our predicament. For better or worse, we were now tied so tightly together that it would be almost impossible to extricate ourselves.

Being permanently and irrevocably bound to him and agreeing to allow him sole access to my body wasn't what was upsetting me. The knowledge that his attraction for me wasn't real and never would be was the cause of my distress. He didn't have the eternal restriction that I'd just placed on myself not to be with another man.

With a wry snort, I shut off the water and got hold of myself. I was no longer a little girl and it was time to grow up. True love might exist, but if it did I obviously wasn't meant to experience it. Instead, I was mated to someone who didn't want me and was forced to protect me due to his loyal nature. I only hoped he never discovered that my feelings for him were genuine.

Reece was waiting in the hall when I opened the door. The look he gave me was guarded and I smiled neutrally. We'd just had mind blowing sex and now we were acting like polite strangers. My breath tried to hitch, but I forced myself to be calm. It wasn't his fault that I loved him and that he'd never feel the same way about me. This was our future now and there was nothing either of us could do to change it.

Chapter Thirty-Three

"Mark wants us to run a final check of the cemeteries before we return to the base," Reece said when we reached the SUV. We hadn't needed the hotel room for the entire night and he'd handed the key over to the receptionist, much to her surprise.

"Okay," I replied. Nightfall was only a couple of hours away now and we spent that time cruising through the city.

When the sun finally set, we began the usual circuit of the graveyards. None showed any signs of green fog and I didn't sense any undead.

Reece saved the cemetery where we'd killed the necromancer last night for last. "I want to make sure the zombies that you sent back to their graves aren't going to rise again," he said. "You can wait in the SUV if you like."

I already knew they were just bones again, but I didn't bother to tell him that and merely nodded. I'd said very little during our search for stray zombies. I felt much better physically, but I was a wreck mentally. Some girls might be able to handle a casual relationship that involved sex without strings, but I wasn't one of them. I could foresee a future where he would be free to pursue any female he liked and would only have sex with me when it was absolutely necessary.

Rage flared at the thought of another female putting her hands on him and I decided I needed fresh air. I hopped out and stretched with my arms up over my head, reaching for the sky. Hearing stealthy footsteps behind me, I whirled around to see Officer Mallory attempting to creep up on me. His expression was crafty and his face was animated with sick excitement.

I wasn't completely sure of his intentions until he leaped forward and slammed me into the SUV. He clamped a hand over my mouth to keep me quiet. "Your boyfriend shouldn't have left you alone," he said with a grin that was pure evil. "You're mine now."

The charming cop was gone and now I saw him for the fiend that he really was. A normal girl would have been frightened, but I was pissed. This man was clearly a monster, but of the human variety. He moved his hand just enough to let me speak. "What are you going to do to me?" I whispered, pretending to be scared. In reality, I was preparing to tear his throat out with my bare hands.

"Everything," he said and ground his pelvis into mine. He was hard and my gorge rose. "Then I'm going to kill you and dump your body in the swamp along with all the other pretty young girls that I've added to my collection over the years."

Reece came out of nowhere with rage pouring off him in waves. "Over my dead body," he growled and wrenched the cop away from me.

I watched with detached amazement as he put his hands around Mallory's neck and squeezed. It took only seconds to pulverize his throat and for the cop to choke on his last breath. I should have been shocked, but all I felt was disappointment that I hadn't had the chance to kill the man.

There were some benefits to being a shifter that I hadn't really thought of. The ability to destroy our enemies without remorse was one of them. Looking down at the crumpled body of the cop, I nudged him with my toe. "Well, he's dead. What now?" We couldn't just leave him there. He'd be found quickly and his death could be traced back to us. Luckily, we'd parked out of range of the CCTV cameras out of habit and the murder hadn't been caught on tape.

"We'll be driving past a swamp on the way back to the base," Reece reminded me.

I smiled at the irony. "Sounds like a plan." Mallory had intended to rape me, kill me and dump me in the marsh. It was fitting that he'd take my place instead.

Reece picked up the body and I opened the back door of the SUV. I helped him to wrap the cop in the blanket that had covered our weapons. When he was snuggled inside, we climbed in and drove away from the city.

A narrow dirt road led us to a series of even narrower tracks. We drove until the road petered out, then parked. Reece didn't need my help to dispose of the body, but I trudged through the boggy ground behind him anyway. Reaching the edge of the swamp, together, we heaved the cop far into the water. Almost immediately, several alligators speared through the murky water towards the blanket wrapped bundle.

"I guess we won't have to worry about our DNA being found," I said as the first reptile reached Mallory.

"Probably not," he agreed.

We drove the rest of the way to the base in silence.

I hadn't eaten much that day and I was starving now that I had my strength back. I headed straight for the kitchen while Reece filled the others in on our activities. He didn't mention Mallory's assault or our side trip to the swamp. He also didn't mention our brief interlude at the hotel.

"What did the priestess have to say?" Mark asked.

Reece's tone was casual when he replied. "The zombies have all been destroyed and the threat no longer remains."

Mark flicked a pointed glance at me. "Did she have any other information?"

Reece knew what he was hinting at. "She said that Lexi would be fine once she leaves New Orleans. Being around the zombies was draining her, but the priestess couldn't explain why."

Our boss didn't quite buy that excuse, but he let the subject drop. I was looking and feeling much better and he was willing to let it slide for now. "We'll head back to Colorado in the morning," he decided. "We've done all we can here and there's no point sticking around any longer."

I was relieved to hear that. Frankly, I hoped I'd never have to see New Orleans again. I had no idea what was going on with me, but I sensed that the priestess was right and that I'd be okay once we left town.

Everyone dispersed after the short meeting. Reece and Flynn disappeared into their bedrooms and Mark retreated to the coms room. Kala took a seat on the couch to watch TV and I joined her when I was finished eating my peanut butter sandwich.

"You look a lot better," she observed.

"I still don't know what was wrong with me," I replied. My hand went to my right shoulder and rubbed it. Realizing what I was doing, I pretended to scratch an itch. I might not know exactly what was wrong, but I knew it had something to do with the fresh bite mark. The story that my dad had told me was a lie. It hadn't been a dog that had bitten me at all, but something far different. A flash of long, dark hair and pale skin came and went. It was hidden behind the strange mental fog that didn't show any signs of dissipating.

"What did you and Garrett really get up to while you were in New Orleans?" she asked. My face went red and her eyes went wide. "You two totally did it!" she crowed, but kept her voice down.

"It's not like we wanted to!" I hissed back.

"Of course you wanted to," she scoffed, then frowned at my miserable expression. "You did want to, didn't you?"

"*I* did, but Reece only did it to save my life. Again." The last word came out sounding bitter.

Scooting over so she could put her arm over my shoulder, she hugged me to her side. "Why don't you start at the beginning and tell Aunty Kala all about it?"

Sniggering at her attempt to sound old and wise, I didn't intend to spill the beans, but I found myself telling her about the fight for my soul and having to strengthen the bond.

She was quiet for a long moment before speaking. "I don't know what is going on with you either, but I think it will be far safer if we leave this place."

I wished we could leave immediately, but Mark had already made the arrangements for the jet to pick us up in the morning. We were stuck here for one more night and the thought filled me with dread.

"There is some good news," I said to distract myself. "I'm not pregnant."

Kala's brows rose in surprise. "How do you know?"

"While we were...together, Reece and I remembered everything that happened after we shifted. We didn't, er, mate," I said awkwardly.

"You remember being werewolves?" she asked in astonishment. I nodded and she scooted back so she could see my face. "What is it like? Are we mindless animals?"

"I think we usually are, but because of our bond, we retained our ability to think and reason like humans. We hunted, but only because we were hungry, not just for the thrill of the chase."

Jealousy came and went and she sagged back against the couch. "You two are so lucky," she said enviously. "I can't remember anything when I shift. I'd give anything to be able to control myself and not turn into a savage beast."

I smiled, but it was cynical. Reece had given up everything when he'd accidentally bitten me and had turned me into a shifter. He was now mentally bonded to me, which meant he might be able to sleep around, but he'd never be able to find his true mate now. I would always be inside his head and he would always be inside mine. We were locked together in a prison that we'd never be free from.

Chapter Thirty-Four

I lay awake for a long time when I went to bed. Eventually, my eyes closed and I drifted off. Minutes or hours later, I heard someone calling my name. When I opened my eyes, I was standing outside. The full moon wasn't even close yet and I looked around in confusion. Had I been sleepwalking again?

A dark, shadowy figure was standing beneath the trees. She was about my height and wore a black dress that fell all the way to her ankles. Her feet were bare. Her hair was long and black and her skin was incredibly pale. Her eyes were shadowed, but I felt them burning into me.

"Alexis," she said and my skin prickled. I'd heard her voice before.

"Who are you?"

She laughed and it sounded like shards of broken glass being crunched beneath booted feet. "You know who I am."

I shook my head in denial and she glided closer. Dressed in a thin singlet and sleeping shorts, I felt undressed and exposed as the woman circled me. There was something very wrong with her, but I couldn't quite put my finger on it. If my mind hadn't been so foggy, I might have been able to figure it out.

"How are you able to resist me?" she asked with a hint of petulance. "It took forever for you to respond to my call this time." Her accent was foreign and might have been European.

I didn't remember anyone calling me, but she must have because I'd left my bed in the middle of the night. I turned to see the building far in the distance.

"Turn around," she ordered in a hard voice.

I complied reluctantly. "What do you want?" I asked.

The question surprised her. She stopped circling me and began to giggle. It was the sound you'd expect to hear from a teenage girl who'd been locked inside an asylum for her entire life. Her crazed, hysterical laughter went on and on until I covered my ears. "Stop it!" I screamed and the sound cut off. The short silence that followed was almost eerie.

"What do you think I want?" she asked. Her voice had changed and it sounded more like a hungry gurgle now.

Catching a glimpse of long, white fangs protruding from her mouth, I shuddered and tried to run.

"Stop!" she commanded and my feet became rooted to the ground. "You are mine, Lexi Levine. You always have and always will belong to me." Her tone spoke of monstrous need. A cold finger trailed from the base of my neck down my spine. It was real this time and I shuddered. "Don't you remember me, sweetheart?"

"No. I don't know who you are." She turned me around and the shadows that had been hiding her face disappeared. For a moment, I thought I was looking into a mirror.

Shock broke the spell that she'd cast to befuddle my wits. I remembered every encounter that I'd had with this evil creature. I remembered her fangs tearing through my skin and my blood being siphoned away twice. No, make that three times. The first time that she'd fed from me, I'd been just a baby. That memory had been locked away until I'd dreamed about it a short time ago. I now knew who she was. The sense of betrayal stunned me and I swayed beneath the force of it.

"Do you remember me now, my darling daughter?" she asked again. Her tone was saccharine sweet. Her affection was a lie, she was only pretending to care about me. The undead weren't capable of love.

"I remember you," I said hoarsely. Her face was so similar to mine that it was startling. She hadn't aged a day in the past eighteen years. She was even more beautiful than in the photo of her that I kept in my locket. A single flaw marred her beauty. A faded, circular scar sat precisely in the center of her otherwise smooth and unlined forehead. To humans, it would have been almost undetectable.

"It's time for you to join me, Alexis," she said. The numbness began to creep over me again as she wormed her way into my mind. My bond with Reece immediately began to weaken. "We can finally be a family again."

Alarm thrummed through the bond as Reece woke and sensed that something was wrong. He sent strength to me through the link. It woke me from the spell again before I could succumb to it completely. With a cry of disgust, I shoved the creature away before her fangs could pierce my flesh again. Hissing with rage, all pretense of affection gone, she swiped her hand at my face. I ducked away before she could claw my eyes out.

Voices sounded in the distance, then someone called my name. It sounded like Mark, but I couldn't be sure. The creature hesitated, then turned to flee. She moved so fast that I could barely track her.

Shaking in reaction, I fell to my knees and hugged myself tightly. I felt sickened as I finally understood the truth that had been hidden from me for my entire life. It hadn't been a dog that had mauled me. My mother might have been murdered when I was a baby, but a human hadn't been responsible for her death. She'd been turned into a soulless monster.

"Oh, my God," I whispered brokenly in heartbreak. "My mother is a vampire!"

New Orleans was her hunting grounds and she'd known who I was the instant that I'd arrived. When my mother had risen from death, she'd returned to the house that she'd shared with my father and had tried to drain me dry. Now that I'd stepped within her clutches after eighteen long years, she was determined to finish the job and to take my life.

The betrayal of my mother trying to kill me was painful enough, but I was almost as wounded by the fact that my father had lied to me. Even after I'd become a supernatural being, he still hadn't told me the truth.

I remembered his wariness when I'd picked him up from the airport and it made even more sense to me now. His wife was a blood sucker and his daughter turned into a wolf at every full moon. Of our small family of three, he was the only human left.

I'd felt a rift form between us from the moment that I'd informed him that I was a shifter. The gap had widened now that I was aware of his untruths. It had just become a chasm that I wasn't sure could ever be repaired.

Printed in Great Britain
by Amazon